I
Reason You Smile

NISHA

NISHA
BLACK LOVE IN THE STRANGEST PLACES

Contents

I Wanna Be The Reason You Smile

Chapter 1: Kyanah

I stared at the sea of boxes that filled the living room of my newly acquired one-bedroom apartment. I was a woman on a mission an hour ago, grabbing boxes from the U-Haul and shoveling them into my apartment like it was nobody's business. Moving off pure adrenaline, I thought I could finish it all, until reality kicked in and I sat down for a break. I had done well but all the heaviest items still needed to be unloaded, along with miscellaneous items that were haphazardly thrown in. My eyes scanned the room until frustration took over. The amount of clutter that surrounded me was giving me anxiety. Standing, I felt the wetness of my shirt hit my back. "Ew!" I didn't like feeling icky, even if it was for a good cause. I half-kicked, half-pushed the boxes to one side of the wall. The rest of the truck needed to be unloaded but that could wait til later. My back hurt, my heart hurt worse, and I was starving. Plus, I needed to change out of this funky ass outfit and freshen up.

My eyes pooled but I refused to let the tears fall.

"Fuck that nigga," I ground through my teeth and sniffled, then grabbed the lone box labeled Pots & Utensils, slicing it open with a boxcutter, smiling when I saw that I had pulled the right one. I grabbed out a few items, along with some dishes.

One thing I did not play about was my cookware. I only had the best because I loved to cook. I wasn't a chef by far, but I loved creating new dishes and the aromas from my meals served as a stress release.

I needed a release now.

Opening the mostly-empty fridge, I spotted the six pack of Coronas I had purchased on the way here. My phone buzzed on the counter behind me but I ignored it.

Probably my sister, Kaliss, asking if I still needed help with the move.

I didn't need shit from anybody.

Slamming the refrigerator door, my body became wracked with rage. How the fuck was I supposed to get my couch, recliner, dresser, nightstand and bed into this place? *He* had helped me get some of the heavy items onto the truck from his house, then one of the guys at U-Haul helped me get the rest, but... Now I had no one.

I took all my shit from his house. I was the one who made that house into a home, and now... Here I was, starting all over again.

Painful memories of how it all went down clouded my mind but I pushed them away. No time to dwell on the past, no matter how recent it was. I needed to move if I wanted this apartment to have any semblance of organization before the night was over.

I would have to take my time getting everything set up, but my heart sank as I thought of how long it was going to take.

I reopened the fridge to distract myself and grabbed the family sized pack of chicken, then stared at it after re-checking the date and peeling back the plastic casing to open it.

My nose burned as the painful memories hit me once again. Why did I buy all this chicken? It was only me now. I tried my best to be the best woman I could be for him and what he do in response? He shitted on me.

Rage swelled up again but I forced it down, turning the faucet onto a warm temperature. I began humming as I started cleaning the first thigh, then I got a better idea.

I stared down at my phone on the counter. "Okay Google, put on some mothafuckin' Mary J!"

I'm sorry, I can't find that selection.

I let out a giggle, feeling myself relax.

"Okay Google, play Mary. J. Blige please!"

Playing Mary J. Blige on YouTube.

I rolled my eyes and immediately sank into the song. After I finished cleaning the pack of chicken, I realized I was missing my oil. Turning 180 degrees to my sink equipped with a freshly purchased dish rack and cleaning items, I washed my hands and dried them, then grabbed my box cutter. Slicing open another box, I grabbed my cooking oil, white rice, and some stove top stuffing. It wasn't much but it would have to do for tonight. I wasn't going out to any store with my body all funky and my hair all over the top of my head. Pretty soon, the whole pack of chicken was seasoned and floured, and my oil was crackling. I slid the first few pieces into the pan then started the water for the rice. I was preparing a large meal, but I figured I could eat the leftovers over the course of a few days.

Grabbing a Corona from the fridge, I popped it open and took a swig. Now in my element, I was jamming to one of my favorite artists and creating some comfort food to calm my raging heart.

Until I heard a few sharp knocks at my front door.

I had just finished flipping the first batch of chicken and it was coming out perfect. Now somebody had to come disturb my vibe.

I sucked my teeth then stalked over, bitter attitude instantly returning.

Whipping the door open, I immediately wished I hadn't.

Three unfamiliar men stood before me, towering over my petite frame. My mouth immediately grew dry.

Though the building I moved to was in a decent area, my city still had a relatively high crime rate and since I was now alone, that put me at risk. My first thought was of the boxcutter I had sitting in my living room but it was too far for me to reach it.

My panic rose until one of them spoke, cracking a silly smile as the words escaped his lips. "Damn girl, you fine and can cook?"

The other two laughed in agreement.

I stared at the one who spoke first. He was brown-skinned with tattoos up his right arm. His small fro was mostly covered by a black fitted cap, and he wore black tee and gym shorts with Adidas slides and black socks that stretched up his calves.

The other two men were similarly adorned, except the middle one was darker skinned with a beard and waves. He wore a jersey and the other was light skinned with locs and sported a white tee. I relaxed when I noted the redness of their eyes and silly demeanors and realized they were high.

"Yes, I can cook," I finally answered. "Is there a problem?"

The first one shook his head while the middle one wearing the jersey stared at me as if mesmerized and the one in the white tee continued to look goofy. "Not at all. Me and my brothers here were just wanting to welcome you to the neighborhood and ask if we might be able to get a plate."

I wrinkled my nose as the other two burst out laughing. "A plate?"

"Told you she wasn't gonna do it, bruh!" the one in the white tee said, and he dapped the first one up. It was obviously an inside joke but now that I saw these men were harmless, the wheels started turning.

"Y'all want a plate, huh? Ain't it supposed to be the other way around?"

The one in the black tee stared at me in marijuana-induced confusion until I broke it down for him.

"When you are welcoming someone to a neighborhood, you bring them a plate, not the other way around."

He stared at me for a few moments until he looked at the guy in the white tee and they both started laughing again.

"But I guess I can make a concession this time." I rolled my eyes.

All three whipped their heads at me. "Huh?" Black tee said, cheesing like a little kid.

I giggled, becoming influenced by their contagious laughter. "Y'all are gonna have to work for it."

"Say less. We're the men for the job."

I put a hand on my hip. "Did y'all see that truck parked near the back door?"

The one in the jersey nodded, still staring.

"Can y'all bring in my furniture?"

Black tee cut back in. "Sheeit, we will bring in your furniture, set that shit up, and help you unpack. Just give us some chicken!" They all shared another laugh.

I noticed the one in the jersey hadn't said a word since our conversation started, but he kept staring at me.

"Okay fellas, get to work then."

I left the door open and returned to my chicken while they hurried down the hall.

As soon as I returned to my kitchenette, a nervous feeling swept through me. I obviously wasn't the best person at reading niggas. What if their offer to help for chicken was a ruse, and they really had sinister intentions? What if they robbed me? Or killed me?

That fear dissipated as two of them walked back in the door carrying my couch less than two minutes later while the one in the jersey directed like he was some kind of boss. "Not that wall, the other one, dummies!" he said to his friends, then looked at me.

His stare caught me off guard because I had been eyeing him while he directed at first, and a warm feeling filled my body. "You want the couch against that wall, right?" He pointed. "So your TV can sit against the other wall and not be affected by the sunlight?"

I was mesmerized by his honey brown eyes at first so I didn't register his question, then my hearing kicked in and I quickly nodded, tearing my eyes away. "Yes, that's fine," I let out hastily and focused on my chicken.

I felt him continuing to stare at me and I realized my abrupt response could have been seen as rude, but I wasn't about to apologize.

Ten minutes later, the first batch of chicken was done and the men had brought in all the rest of the items from the truck. I only wanted them to move the big things but I couldn't deny I was grateful for their gesture.

They set up my kitchen table, and the one in the jersey had once again directed them on how to angle it for maximum space. I kept my attention on the food as they worked, but my body kept heating up whenever he was around. The man was looking at me like he wanted to get to know me, but I didn't want to know him.

One time I felt him staring and I scrunched my face up in a frown to ward him off. He seemed puzzled but went back to work. I busied myself by fixing their plates. They only had one piece of chicken each since I only had time to make one batch, but the second batch was sizzling on the stove.

"Damn, this is good," Black tee said, smacking heavily as he ate.

The other two nodded, then the one in the jersey sat back and fixed me with a solid gaze. Why was he still looking at me? I thought my telepathic message from earlier had gone through. Apparently not. His honey brown eyes were even more penetrating from a shorter distance, and his full lips that were surrounded by well-groomed mustache and a perfectly crafted beard almost caused me to swoon. He wasn't wearing a hat like the others, so I was able to see that his waves were immaculately done too. My heart dropped to my panties, then I angled my body so I wasn't facing him directly. "What's your name?" he asked. His voice was smooth and sexy, as were the lips he spoke from, but I refused to allow that thought to fester.

For some reason, him asking my name killed my vibe. A niggling feeling grew in the back of my mind but I squelched it. I was attracted to this man, that I couldn't deny, but it was way too soon to be entertaining another potential heartache.

"Does it matter?" I asked in a ruder tone than I meant. "Y'all are just here for a simple transaction, right?" I tore my eyes away from him and focused on my plate. Silence consumed the rest of the table as the other two enjoyed their meal while staring back and forth between me and Mr. Jersey.

He didn't respond so I glanced back at him and caught the incredulous glint in his eyes. "Damn, what if I just wanted to know how to greet you?"

I didn't want him greeting me, especially not with those lips or those eyes, but I forced a neutral tone as I responded. "Kyanah."

"Kyanah," White tee said as he licked his fingers, then he looked at the boxes strewn all over my floor before focusing back on me. "Yo, I got another proposition for you."

I already knew where this was going, seeing that his plate was clean except for the chicken bone and he eyed those boxes like they would bring him his next meal, but I entertained him anyway. "Yes?"

"How many more pieces of chicken can we get if we unpack your boxes for you?"

Black tee let out a playful chuckle as if getting on his friend for being greedy, but he looked at me with intrigue too.

The one in the jersey seemed turned off, which was fine by me.

I opened my mouth to answer, but Jersey turned to face me and cut me off before I could say anything. "Why doesn't Kyanah have her man help her unpack the boxes? I think we've overstayed our welcome as it is."

I focused on flipping the second batch of chicken as I answered. "Obviously I don't have a man; otherwise, why would y'all be here?"

"Maybe if you weren't so rude to people, you would..."

I whipped my head around to give him a piece of my mind but White tee cut in between us, holding his hands up. "Let's get back to the matter at hand. Kiki, how are you feeling, baby girl? I can do this shit myself to be honest. How many pieces of chicken can I get for unpacking all this shit for you?"

I couldn't help but roll my eyes at his antics, my anger at his friend dissipating. "Oh, so I'm Kiki now huh? You laying it on thick, Sir. I'll tell you what: help me get all the boxes in the right rooms and I will unpack them myself. Then you can have as many pieces of chicken as you want."

"Bet," he said, and jolted from his seat before either of the other two men could say anything.

After he got up, Black tee rose from his seat to help and they didn't have to ask me where each box went. I had them all labeled so it was easy to tell, and the miscellaneous items were obvious enough to know where they should be placed too.

Jersey continued to stare at me as I pretended to be busy with the chicken.

"Guess I'll wash my plate," he said, and slowly stood.

He dumped his chicken bone in the trash, then strode toward me. As he approached the mini kitchenette that was only big enough to house the stove, fridge, and then cabinets and sink across from it, I remembered how tall he was. And I caught the musky scent of his cologne. My breath hitched as we stood toe to toe with him towering over me.

"May I approach your sink or are you guarding that like you did your name?"

My eyes widened at his question. "What do you mean? I'm not guarding anything."

I stepped aside and he grabbed my empty plate which I ate while standing across from the stove and began washing both of our dishes, placing them in the dish rack when finished.

I stared at him the whole time, but when he turned to look back at me, I busied myself by using my cooking fork to pluck the second batch of chicken out of the pan.

"Kyanah..." he said, and my heart skipped a beat at how close he was standing and how my name sounded rolling off his lips, but his boys bounded back into the kitchen area, interrupting us. White tee's eyes widened. "It's done?" he asked, when he saw me holding the plate.

I giggled. He was too silly. I quickly fixed him a new plate with two pieces along with some more rice and stuffing, then did the same for Black tee.

I turned to Jersey, who was now leaning against my counter, seeming to enjoy how uncomfortable he made me feel by being this close in such a cramped space.

"You don't want any more?" I tried to say it nicely, but it came out more like an accusation.

"Nope. I'm good," he said while his friends greedily scarfed down my food, cursing as they burnt their tongues eating the fresh-out-the-pan chicken.

I tried not to show it, but I was offended by the fact that he didn't want more chicken. I prided myself on my cooking skills, and part of me felt like his rejection was done because he was proving some kind of point.

I began unpacking boxes in my living room, partially to keep my eyes on the men in case they tried anything. If they did, what was I going to do? There were three of them and one of me. But in my heart, I knew there was no reason to fear them. They had already moved all my stuff in as they said they would, and I still had my box cutter if anything popped off. But I knew it wouldn't. They were high and wanted to work for some chicken, that was all. Well, the first two did, but the one in the Jersey was eating at me. Couldn't he tell I didn't want to be bothered?

The final batch of chicken was still cooking, so I kept an eye out for that too. The men chatted in the kitchen as they ate, but my mind stayed on Jersey. What was his deal? Why did he keep staring at me? And why were his actions making me feel the way they did? I didn't know him from a brick in the wall. And I didn't want to get to know him either. I re-entered the kitchenette to take out the last batch of chicken, and White tee eyed me as I did so, so I playfully rolled my eyes and gave him another piece and added one to Black tee's plate too before he could even ask.

Jersey was staring at me too, but I refused to look at him as I wrapped the rest of the chicken and sides in aluminum foil and put them in the fridge. I washed my hands and dried them, then returned to the living room to continue unpacking boxes. Halfway through the second box, I heard the water running amidst the chatter from White tee and Black tee. They were growing mighty comfortable in my kitchen. Jersey was at the sink, washing my cast iron skillet. I sucked my teeth and moved to get up but sank back down a second later. If he wanted to wash it, whatever. After he washed it, I couldn't help but notice him re-oil it too. That simple act caused my heart to flutter, but I quickly focused back on my boxes like I didn't see him.

Soon, the others were done eating and I heard their plates clattering into the sink.

I re-entered the kitchen to face them. White tee approached me. "Kyanah, that was the best chicken I ever had in my life." He emphasized his words with his hands as he spoke. "If you ever, and I mean ever, need anything else moved or even a handyman, I'm up in 412. Hit me. I'm Tremaine."

I shook my head at his silliness. "Thank you, Tremaine. I might take you up on that."

"Thanks Kiki," Black tee said, stealing Tremaine's nickname for me. "I'm Los. You can call me too."

I rolled my eyes and waited for Jersey to come forward and tell me his name, but he didn't. He walked out the door with his boys and closed it in my face.

What the hell?

I know this nigga did not just close my own door on me!

I had half a mind to wrench it back open and curse him out but decided against it.

Wasn't like we knew each other anyway, and since this building had five floors, I would make it a point to avoid him at all costs.

Chapter 2: Kendrix

Tremaine and Los ragged on each other the whole elevator ride up to our floor. But my mind was on Kyanah. I couldn't help but to admit she was fine as hell with her cocoa butter skin, slim-thick frame, and wild curly hair with the chinky eyes, but I wasn't getting caught up in that shit. Typical bitter female. A brother tried to be cordial, and all she came back with was attitude.

What crawled up her ass?

I contemplated it as my stomach grumbled. I did want some more chicken when Kyanah offered, but somebody needed to teach our new neighbor a lesson about manners. Well, Tremaine and Los' new neighbor - I was only staying here til I got back on my feet. I declined the chicken because I caught the look of pride in her eyes when Tremaine and Los bragged about how good it was. She needed to be knocked down a peg or two.

My phone buzzed with a text, jarring me from my thoughts. *Thank you, baby,* my mom had texted. She must have just seen the Cash App I sent her for her mortgage. I had been paying my mom's mortgage ever since my father passed a few years ago. She was a widow and was living off Dad's life insurance policy, but I knew the money wouldn't last forever, so I helped her out.

You don't have to thank me, Ma, I responded.

How are you feeling? You know you can always come with me.

That was where I drew the line. I loved my mother and it would be perfectly logical to move back in with her since I was paying the mortgage anyway, but I was a grown ass man. I hadn't lived with my parents since I moved out as a teenager and I didn't plan on moving back now.

I'm good, Ma. Thank you though.

You're coming Sunday, right? I'm cooking.

I cheesed as I responded. *You know I am.* That was another thing my mother never had to question. It was her and my father's ritual to go to church together every Sunday, and I had served as her escort ever since he passed.

That girl never took care of you like she was supposed to anyway.

My smile erased at that message, and hurtful memories sliced through my mind about why I was here with Tremaine and Los rather than at my own place, but I pushed them away. My stomach grumbled again.

The slow-ass elevator finally arrived on our floor. The bell dinged and Tremaine and Los looked at me and snickered.

"Fuck y'all laughing at?"

Tremaine lifted his chin. "Why you ain't want no more chicken?"

Los snickered again. "'Cause Kyanah's ass curved him, that's why."

I let them share a hearty laugh at my expense, but I wasn't one to give up easy when it came to verbal sparring. "That girl ain't curve shit. Plus nobody was trying to talk to her anyway. She's obviously bitter."

We walked down the hall toward their apartment. "She seemed cool to me," Tremaine said.

"And she can cook," Los added. "Kendrix, you might as well try to get in good with her so she can make us some more chicken."

"Why don't you have your girl cook?" I teased.

Los sucked his teeth. "Who, Tracey? That girl can barely boil water. I never told y'all about the time she called herself cooking for me and I came home to some damn boxed noodles, instant mashed potatoes, and fully-cooked steak."

"Fully cooked steak?" Tremaine wrinkled his nose. "Where do they sell that?"

Los corrected himself. "Well it wasn't fully cooked but it was pre-seasoned. And she still somehow dried it out."

Los and Tremaine continued to rag on Tracey's cooking while I discreetly opened my phone to order food. My ribs were touching and I couldn't get the taste of Kyanah's chicken out of my mouth.

My mind went to another place as I imagined what she tasted like rather than her chicken but I stopped it.

That was never happening.

Tremaine flipped on the TV and Los rolled some more weed and offered me some. I declined and they started getting on me again, but I tuned them out.

When my food came, Los and Tremaine immediately dug in the bag like I ordered for them too but I didn't say shit because they let me live in their place rent free until I struck out again on my own.

I didn't plan to stay here long. All I needed was to regroup, get my mind right, and move on from the bullshit I just went through.

Chapter 3: Kyanah

I broke down all the boxes in my living room and bedroom, but the kitchen and bathroom would have to wait til later, along with hanging my wall art and the rest of my decor.

The whole time I was working, my mind was on Tremaine and Los' friend... or was he their brother? The three men sort of favored one another and they said they were brothers when they introduced themselves, but that could have been slang for the fact that they were close friends.

Why didn't he want to tell me his funky ass name?

Whatever, I didn't need to know anyway.

Still, I couldn't get him out of my mind.

My nose wrinkled as I thought of the fact that I was attracted to a man who came to my door, high, asking for a plate of chicken.

"Ew, Kyanah. Desperate ass." I shunned myself.

Not that I was against people smoking weed, but I was not about to entangle myself with a pothead. Especially a lazy one. He didn't lift a finger to help his cousins or brothers or whoever the hell they were with moving my stuff. The most he did was direct like he owned my damn apartment instead of me.

He also didn't ask for more chicken, my mind reminded me, but he only did that out of spite. Still, his spite proved whatever point he was trying to make. He hit me where it hurt and gave me something to think about. I was rude to him for no reason when it was obvious he was trying to help.

"Whatever," I repeated, convincing myself that I would be over him by morning. The man looked good, I would give him that, but looks weren't everything. I shuddered as my heart stung with the memory of why I knew that firsthand.

No more time for depressing thoughts. I was starting a new life and things would get better for me soon.

Since I left my previous residence in haste, I had hella laundry that needed to be done. Thankfully none of the men made mention of my funky ass clothes in my laundry bags. The building had a laundry room on the first floor, which was where I lived. I would drag my bags over in the morning. Hopefully if I got inside early enough I could beat whatever crowd would surely ensue with there being only one laundry room in the entire building. Did the laundry room take cards or coins? I hoped it took cards because I never carried cash on me. I sucked my teeth at the thought of having to go to the ATM early in the morning before I washed my clothes.

I made a mental note to check the room as soon as I woke up and hopefully the machines took cards.

Then my mind went to whether all the machines would be in good condition - I did not want to be held up all day restarting dryers that moved at a glacial pace to finish loads - then a call from my sister interrupted my thoughts.

I contemplated not answering, but sucked my teeth and pressed the green button. I had avoided her enough today. "Hello?" I answered, full of attitude as I laid on my back on my bed, staring at the ceiling.

"Hello to you too," Kaliss clapped back, matching my energy. "Did you say you were moving today or tomorrow?"

"I moved today, Kaliss."

She gasped. "What? Why didn't you tell me?"

"Because you didn't need to know. I'm clearly by myself in this world anyway. Fuck can you do for me?"

Kaliss was silent for a long time. "Listen, I know you're upset sis, but you have to understand my position."

"Mm hm, yup, I fully understand," I let out in a sarcastic tone, cutting her off. "You couldn't fix your lips to say anything to me, yet you knew what was going on behind my back. Yup, I gotcha, sis."

Kaliss fell silent again. "You know what? I'm going to call you tomorrow."

"Yup." I hung up before she could say another word, then slammed my phone onto my nightstand and turned away, a fresh set of tears streaming down my cheeks.

Chapter 4: Kendrix

Damn! Who the fuck was in the laundry room this early? I sucked my teeth as I carried my bag down the hall toward the room which sounded like it was full of activity.

Tremaine and Los assured me that six o'clock in the morning was the perfect time to do laundry because nobody would be in there.

Now look at my luck.

I hoped whoever was in there only used one or two washers because my clothes had to be done before I went to work.

When I made it to the open doorway that housed the room, my heart dropped. Kyanah was busy putting her clothes in the second to last washer. She hadn't noticed me yet, which gave me time to think. Did I want to deal with her today? Our last encounter left much to be desired and I didn't want some bitter female yelling in my ear early in the morning. As I was about to leave, she caught me out of the corner of her eye and jumped, almost tripping over her feet. "What the hell is wrong with you?" she said with accusatory eyes.

I scrunched my face. "What do you mean, what's wrong with me?"

Her eyes narrowed further. "You've been standing there watching me for how long?"

One of my lips curled in disgust. "Nobody has time to stand around watching you. If you haven't noticed, which obviously you haven't since you took almost every washer in the mothafucka, this is a public laundry room. A place designated for all residents to use."

At those words, she quickly refocused on her laundry, but her cheeks reddened as if my words stung her. Now I felt bad. I was about to apologize for my harsh tone when she pressed the button to start her washer then focused back on me, her expression etched in stone.

"Well, you got lucky. Your bag of laundry should fit in the last washer." With those words, she stalked past me out of the room, bumping my arm as she walked.

I wanted to stop her and apologize since we got off on a negative foot and I didn't like having unnecessary drama in my life, but part of me was unwilling to move.

I entered the room and put my clothes in the final washer - Kyanah was right, they fit - but my conscience wouldn't let me rest.

She's obviously going through something, one side of my mind said. *So what?* The other side chimed in. *Aren't we all?* I had my own situation I was dealing with to be focused on trying to make friends with somebody who was dead set on being negative. I was about to say fuck it, then I noticed that Kyanah had left her laundry detergent on top of one of the washers. It was the expensive kind too - maybe that was my opening. I could bring it to her, apologize, then we could be friendly neighbors from this day forward. I grabbed the detergent with a chuckle, reasoning that it was unlikely we would be friendly neighbors, but at least her attitude would die down. I halted in my tracks when she re-entered the room, her jaw dropping when she saw what I was holding.

"Now you're stealing my shit?"

"What? Nobody's..."

She stalked over and snatched it from my hands. "Buy your own laundry detergent. This one is mine."

I stared at her, perplexed. "What is wrong with you?"

She put a hand on her hip. "Ain't nothing wrong with me."

"Obviously there is if all I've seen you display is attitude in the two times we've seen each other. What's going on? You need some dick or something?"

As soon as I said that, I knew I crossed a line. Her face flashed with an indiscernible expression before it switched to anger. "Excuse me?" She rolled her neck as she spoke. "I don't know what gave you the impression that I'm hard up for a nigga, but as you saw last night, I can handle shit on my own pretty well."

I wasn't going down a rabbit hole with her since I still wanted us to get off on the right foot. "Look, I didn't mean to offend you, but you really need to loosen up. What's wrong with you?"

Kyanah rolled her eyes. "If I wanted a therapist I would sign up with a qualified professional. Mind your business, please and thank you."

With those words, she whirled around and exited the room, leaving me lost in my contemplations.

Chapter 5: Kyanah

A few weeks later...

I stared at the summons until my eyes blurred. This was pure bullshit. That bitch was suing me? How dare she? I had barely begun to pick up the pieces of my life after using vacation time from my job to get settled into my new place, and now the bitch was suing?

I had half a mind to call her but decided against it. It would likely only make things worse. It was bad enough I was arrested and spent a night in jail after being blindsided by treachery, but now the situation was being dragged out and made worse.

Our court date was swiftly approaching and I had been spending the last couple of weeks putting the incident out of my mind, but this summons made it come crashing back to reality. What possible grounds could she have to sue? The fucking audacity...

I shook my head and my first thought was to call my lawyer-sister, Kaliss, but I stopped myself before I could tap her name in my phone. Fuck Kaliss, she was part of the reason I was in this predicament. If she had said something to me before the whole situation blew up in my face, I would have known, and I wouldn't have...

My eyes pooled and at first I was going to force my tears back, but I said fuck it and let them fall. I was alone in this world as it was. Why not let the pain seep through? Everybody said there was healing in letting out your emotions, right? I needed to let myself grieve so I could move on.

That thought re-angered me. It would be much easier to move on without this court date and lawsuit hanging over my head. I wanted to be done with this shit, but now I would have to wait to see what the judge said. Hopefully he or she would see what I went through and have mercy on me.

"Have mercy on me..." I sang, then told Google to play "Many Men", by 50 Cent. I was in a gutter type of mood and listening to hardcore rap was one of the ways I blew off steam besides cooking.

Matter of fact, I needed to see what was in my refrigerator. My stomach was grumbling and a comfort meal would do me good. I went grocery shopping the other day, so some smothered pork chops, baked macaroni and cheese, and green beans were about to be on the menu.

I had been consuming quite a few comfort meals lately, and sooner or later, I would get a grip, but for now, I was letting myself go.

Halfway to the refrigerator, pain filled my heart and I collapsed to the floor, sobbing my eyes out and punching the floor as the memories of what transpired filled my mind.

I laid there on the floor, allowing 50's smooth but gritty tone to fill my eardrums as I took in the words of the song.

By the time "Many Men" finished playing, I felt better. I sat up. This bullshit would not get the best of me. I was going to stand up, dust my shoulders off, and find a way to move forward. Plenty of people did it all the time. I wasn't the first person on this earth to get done dirty in the worst way, and some people's stories were even worse than mine.

I took a few deep breaths, then slowly rose to my feet as "As We Ride" by Tupac played next on the playlist.

Chapter 6: Kendrix

I headed home after a long day's work, wanting nothing more than to eat, shower, then become dead to the world for a few hours. I hadn't been sleeping well lately. It was a sign of stress, but I wasn't ready to deal with it yet.

I parked my car and sat for a moment, staring at the building in front of me. This was not how shit was supposed to go. I was supposed to be married, possibly working on a seed by now. Not sleeping on my boys' couch while trying to piece my life back together after the ultimate betrayal.

Sucking my teeth, I forced the negative thoughts back to the crevices of my mind then stepped out of my car. After stretching and letting out a groan, I headed toward the front steps of the building.

There was a familiar frame standing at the front door. A female. Wearing a red, curve-hugging t-shirt and short ensemble, equipped with red Converse. Her hair was out and her curls splayed wildly all over her head. From the looks of it, she was having trouble jiggling the lock to get the security door open, but I wasn't focused on that. My gaze was zeroed in on her ass.

My dick jumped at the sight of it and my mouth grew dry. I swallowed and approached her. If I hadn't been thinking and seeing with the wrong head, I would have noticed it was Kyanah's bitter ass and not another one of the other ladies who lived in the building.

When I recognized it was her, I stopped short. Did I really wanna deal with this today?

She stomped in frustration, and that was when I stepped forward and opened the outer door so I could help her.

When I entered the small area between the outer door and the security door, Kyanah sensed my presence and turned around. Her eyes lit up at first, then scrunched into a frown.

"Hello to you too," I said, trying to keep the mood neutral but still irritated at the fact that she always gave me attitude for no reason.

Before she could open her mouth to sass me, I reached out and covered her hand with mine. "Need some help?"

She flinched and her features reddened at my touch and I couldn't front that I felt a tingling sensation too. But that shit was dead before it started. She would never give me any play and I didn't want any either.

Instead of answering my question, Kyanah stepped back and I stepped forward, expertly maneuvering the key so that the door unlocked.

"They really need to fix this shit," I remarked, handing her back her key chain and holding the door open for her.

She stared at me as if forcing a grateful expression. "They do. Thanks."

I wanted to say something more to her, but she quickly walked inside and bounded down the stairs toward her floor while my floor was up the stairs.

So much for neighborly conversation.

Chapter 7: Kyanah

I tried my best not to let the shit I was going through cause me to lash out at others, but it seemed I couldn't help myself around him. I still didn't know his name, but whenever I saw him, it always seemed to be at the wrong moment.

I started my day at court, finding out about that bullshit lawsuit the bitch took out on me. After I left there, I came home and changed, then went out to get myself some ice cream for comfort, but it wasn't comforting. I ate at the restaurant, but wasted most of my cone, lamenting about that trifling ass nigga.

His bitch stood in front of that judge and gave an Oscar-worthy performance, crying and talking about how she feared for her life and safety since I attacked her, and how I endangered her baby because she was pregnant.

I hadn't known the bitch was pregnant, but now that I did know, it twisted the dagger.

Kaliss had told me to tell her when the court date was, but fuck her. Yeah, she was a lawyer, but she could have helped me prevent this situation from the beginning. Plus apparently I was pretty good at advocating for myself. The judge didn't give me any serious charges. She sentenced me to pay a fine and get anger management.

Now I had to pay a bitch who betrayed me and go to weekly meetings to apologize for an ass-whooping that was well deserved.

My mind went back to that day but I couldn't let it fester.

I had other things to worry about, like how I had to rearrange my schedule to accommodate the anger management meetings.

I entered my apartment with a sigh, then closed the door and locked it.

Finally, some alone time.

I told Google to play some music, then went on the internet and scrolled social media to take my mind off my current depressing life.

This was not how things were supposed to be. Terrance and I were supposed to get married, have our own children, and be starting our life as a family.

But apparently the nigga never felt the same way for me that I did for him.

I was a fool. How did I not see the signs that something wasn't right? How did the revelation of what was going on take me so far out of character that I got into a fistfight? I was never one to throw hands, though I could hold my own. But when I found out what happened, it caught me off guard in the worst way.

I never would have thought in a million years that he would betray me like that. Especially not with her. Technically, she owed me no loyalty since he was my man, but she sat there and played in my face for God knows how long. Judging from how it went down, they were together for most, if not all our relationship.

What did I do to deserve that? I cooked for him, helped him with work tasks, encouraged him, made love to him... I did everything a woman could to please her man and he played me.

I didn't understand.

Chapter 8: Kendrix

I showed up bright and early on Sunday to escort my mother to church. I strode up to her front door, but she opened it before I could knock, wearing her pink skirt-suit, equipped with a pink purse, kitten heels, and a wide-brimmed hat. I always loved how my mother dressed for church. She had a skirt-suit and hat ensemble in every color, and she always carried peppermints in her purse for me. I couldn't deny I still liked how she offered them to me even as a grown ass man. I would cheese and take one just how I did as a kid, and she would give me a loving smile. It was our ritual, just like her and Dad going to church together on Sundays was their ritual.

"Good morning, son!" she said, and extended her arms to give me a hug.

I stooped to embrace her smaller frame, catching a whiff of her perfume. She always wore the same kind, ever since I was a child.

After our hug, I extended my arm so she could take it, and we walked down the steps toward my freshly cleaned car. I opened the door for her and closed it after she was inside, then strode around to the driver's seat and clicked my seatbelt.

The old school gospel radio station was already playing, and Ma was tapping her feet to "He's Alright" while nodding her head to the beat.

I smiled and put my blinker on to pull away from the curb.

We rode mostly in silence, then when we entered the church parking lot, I pulled up close to the door so Ma could get out and not have to walk too far. Some of her friends – the other mothers of the church – were congregated outside, and they began a lighthearted conversation while I parked.

When I approached them, the group of elderly women gave me knowing smiles.

"Hey Mother Theresa, Mother Sue." I greeted each of them with a hug.

Mother sue kept her hand on my shoulder after our hug and looked up at me. "You're such a handsome young man. Shame you're still single."

I chuckled. "Well, I'm waiting on the Lord for my wife," I replied. Not because I was actively looking for a wife, but because it would be the quickest way to get her off my back.

Mother Theresa's eyes lit up. "You know Deacon Clarence's daughter is available. Pretty young thang, ain't y'all the same age?"

I grew tongue-tied. "I'm not sure," I said, and moved to walk toward the building.

Mother Theresa persisted. "I could get her phone number for you if you'd like."

I gave her a polite smile and shook my head. "Thank you, Ma'am, but no thanks. I would rather approach a woman on my own."

"Don't take too long, now," Mother Sue said. "You know your mother wants some grandbabies."

At those words, my heart faltered. I forced a smile back and said, "Yes ma'am. One of these days I'll have a whole house full."

That seemed to appease them, and we entered the building. My mother always sat in the second row, the Mother's section, but she wanted me next to her like Dad used to be. We sat in our seats and waited for the service to start.

I tried to pay attention but couldn't help drifting off into a not-so-distant memory.

***

It had been over a month since it happened, but the memory still rang through my brain. Me and Jazzmyne were in love, or at least I thought we were. When I first met her, she was in the department store parking lot, struggling to lift an air conditioner out of her cart to put it in her trunk.

Never one to see a woman struggle and not jump in to help, I approached her. "You good?" I asked, then before she could answer, I lifted it out of the cart and gently laid it into her nearly empty trunk. The few items that were in the trunk were action figures. That let me know she must have had a son.

A quick glance through her rear windshield confirmed that for me when she slammed the trunk and thanked me. "I appreciate you," she said, giving me an alluring smile.

My heart thumped in my chest. "No doubt." I was about to walk away since I had completed my good deed, but something about this woman's eyes made me want to get to know her.

"I'm Kendrix," I announced, and she was about to turn away too before a look of surprise crossed her features.

"Jazzmyne," she responded.

I gestured toward the car. "You grabbed that AC for you and little man, huh?"

Her eyes widened again before she relaxed into a smile. "Yup. They said a heat wave is coming."

"Shit, I might need an AC myself. You just gave me a good idea."

We stared at each other for a few moments, and I was about to walk away because it didn't seem that she was interested in my conversation, then she spoke again. "How can I repay you for helping me?" Back was the alluring smile that drew me in from the beginning.

I licked my lips. "You can let me take you out sometime."

Her smile widened, and we exchanged numbers.

On our first date, I learned that her son, Kanai, was four years old and her baby father was locked up doing a fifteen-year bid for hustling.

When I first heard that, I was reluctant to continue dating her, but Jazzmyne assured me that he had already been locked up for three years and they hadn't had any contact since he went in.

That helped me relax a little, though the information still played with my mind.

Another source of reluctance came from the fact that she had a son and I knew they were a package deal. I didn't have any kids, though I wanted some.

After our date, I did some thinking, but before the week was out, Jazzmyne offered for me to come over for her to cook me dinner.

At first I was going to say no, but decided to give her a chance. The woman couldn't help the situation she was in. It wasn't her fault her baby daddy went to prison a year after her son was born.

I gave in.

When I arrived at her apartment, I was pleased by what I saw. Everything was neat and in order and the way she organized and decorated the place reminded me of my mom. Everything about Jazzmyne screamed that she was a good woman who had a great head on her shoulders and was going places. This was someone I could build with.

Or so I thought.

The dinner was great and Jazzmyne surprised me at the end of the evening when her cousin, the babysitter, brought Kanai home.

I was told he would be spending the night at her cousin's house, but apparently, the cousin had some kind of emergency so she had to bring him home early.

That made me nervous because although I was feeling Jazzmyne, this was only our first official date.

Jazzmyne gave me an apologetic smile. "So sorry," she said. "I'll put him to bed."

Kanai stared up at me with wide eyes and it touched my soul. "Mommy, who's your friend?"

For some reason, one look in that little boy's eyes was all it took for me to fall in love. I wanted to step in and be his father figure. I had seen too many stories of young boys who slipped through the cracks and ended up on the wrong side of the law because they had no guidance.

This little boy was so full of light. I wanted to keep it shining.

I knelt to his level. "I'm Kendrix," I said, staring into his eyes.

He grinned at me and that was when I noticed one of his teeth was missing. "Hi Kendis!"

I laughed and gave him a kiddie dap.

"Wanna see Spiderman?" he asked, and I was about to say yes, but Jazzmyne cut in.

"Kanai, honey, it's time for you to go night-night."

I looked up at her from my kneeling position and she winked down at me, then led her son to his bedroom.

I busied myself by rinsing our dishes, then loading them into the dishwasher while she put her son to sleep.

When she returned to the kitchen, it was on. I knew it from the coy stare she fixed on me as she sauntered forward like she was ready for action.

I grew nervous because Kanai was in the other room.

As if hearing my thoughts, Jazzmyne said, "He's knocked out and won't be back up until morning."

That was all I needed to hear, especially since she was pressed up against me now. My manhood was growing and eager to meet her.

I stared down into her eyes, speaking in a husky tone. "You ready for this?"

She chuckled. "What you mean, am I ready for it? Are you ready for me, is the better question."

I licked my lips, my heart skipping a beat at her confidence. "Alright now, don't start no shit you can't handle."

She looked me up and down. "Trust me, you ain't saying nothing but a thing."

Seconds later, we were on each other like white on rice. A series of movements and flinging clothing, then moments later, we were inside her bedroom and she was calling my name as I plunged inside of her.

I kept my promise to give her some shit that would make her toes curl and eyes roll back, and she returned the favor when we finished by swallowing me whole.

"Damn, Ma, you wasn't playing," I said when she climbed back up my body after she finished.

She licked her lips. "Like I told you before, I don't have time for games." She stared into my eyes. "You think you can handle a woman like me?"

I stared back at her, my vision growing hazy from the session we just had. "As long as we keep it real with each other, I think we can make it work."

It was settled from that night, or so I thought.

***

Our relationship lasted three years until it all crumbled last month. I had been growing increasingly frustrated and suspicious of Jazzmyne for a while. About six months prior, she started acting funny.

I hinted at the idea of us sealing the deal and getting married since our relationship had progressed so well. I also wanted to broach the idea of us trying for another baby since Kanai was doing great and had been asking for a baby brother or sister.

It was like as soon as I dropped hints about us taking things to the next level, Jazzmyne started pulling back.

A look flitted across her features like she was disgusted by my suggestion. That twisted me up because it wasn't the first time she gave me a look like that even though she played it off the first time.

"Something wrong?" I asked, tensing for a fight.

Jazzmyne turned her head. "How are we going to get married when we don't even have a house yet, Kendrix?"

That threw me for a loop because she never mentioned us getting a house before. I had moved into her apartment and taken over the rent and all the household bills, so all she had to do was spoil herself and Kanai with her money.

My job as a forklift driver of a local warehouse paid pretty well, though I wasn't a rich man. I could afford to pay all the bills and take her on a few mini vacations, which was all Jazzmyne initially said she wanted. But as our relationship grew, so did her demands.

Never one to back down from a challenge, especially when it involved my woman, I rose to the occasion, negotiating a higher raise than my job initially offered and putting in a couple hours of overtime each week so I could afford the clothes, shoes, and bags she increasingly wanted. I didn't see a need for all those outfits when we didn't go out much, but if it made my woman happy, I was ready to provide.

But a house would need more preparation and timing. My credit was straight and I had a few thousand in the bank but if we wanted to do this right I needed a lot more money.

I immediately increased my overtime hours. Soon, I was working twelve hours a day, six days a week because I wanted to save for a house and an engagement ring at the same time. According to my calculations, with my salary, six months was all it would take to get it done.

Until the week I planned to propose. I came home to a sight that stopped my world.

***

I knew something was wrong the moment I saw the shiny red Corvette parked outside. No one we knew drove that type of vehicle.

Thrown for a loop, I was about to call Jazzmyne when I noticed her car was parked in one of the visitor's spaces.

My face scrunched in confusion. Why was she parked in a visitor's space? The landlords allowed each unit two spaces in front of their apartments.

A weird feeling passed through me, like I knew something was about to go down, but I couldn't figure out what it was.

Numbness filled my body as I put my key into the lock and twisted it, turning the lock to open the front door.

I immediately saw the source of the red Corvette sitting on the couch that I recently purchased, playing one of my video games with Kanai.

Who was this nigga?

Sensing my presence, he turned around, and that was when the weight of what was happening hit my chest.

He cracked a smile as if he were expecting me. It wasn't the friendly type of smile, more like the kind where a man silently told another man that he was invading on his territory.

Standing, he faced me. "So you're him, huh?"

I usually wasn't the type to curse in front of Kanai but at that moment I couldn't help but to let one out as my mind started having flashbacks of the past six months and connecting dots I didn't know existed.

"Nigga, who the fuck are you?" I asked, but I already knew. The man was the older version of Kanai. It had to be Sky, Kanai's father. According to Jazzmyne, the man should have had at least nine years left in his sentence, but apparently, she had gotten the math wrong.

At that moment, Jazzmyne emerged from the kitchen wearing a robe. Her hair was messed up when she had just got it done yesterday, and the look of slight embarrassment when she saw me let me know that she had fucked him.

Taking a few moments to catch her words, Jazzmyne spoke to me. "Kendrix, you're home early."

"Warehouse shut down," I shot back. Shutdowns happened from time to time when a major piece of equipment became damaged or the employees participated in scheduled cleaning days. My fist curled at my side. This shit was not about to end well because Jazzmyne was still looking at me like she was stuck on stupid.

"Kendrix, Daddy's home!" Kanai said, seemingly oblivious to the tension in the room.

Sky hadn't said another word since me and Jazzmyne started talking, but he was staring at me with his arms crossed, wearing a smirk like they had been planning this interaction for a while.

"I see that, little man," I responded, my heart faltering for a second. If what I thought was about to happen happened, I would never see him again.

"Baby, go to your room for a second," Jazzmyne said, staring between me, Sky, and her son.

Kanai put up a fight. "Mommy, we're not finished!" He held up his controller.

She gave me another quick look, then turned back to her son. "You and Daddy will finish in a minute. Go ahead to your room and I'll call you when it's time to come out."

Kanai looked at me with a hopeful expression. "Kendrix, will you play with me and Daddy too?"

A tear formed in the corner of my eye. I couldn't answer him.

"Go on," Jazzmyne urged, and Kanai raced off to his room. When his door closed, she turned to me. "I thought you would be home later."

"Why does it matter?" I shot back, my anger growing by the second now that Kanai was out of earshot. "Did you want to freshen up from your fuck session before you told me you were getting back with your baby father?"

I turned to him. "You let another nigga take care of your girl and your son while you sat in prison?"

Sky bucked up like what I had just said offended him. "Nigga, you ain't take care of shit. My girl and our son were well taken care of by me while I was on the inside. You were just something to do while I was gone. I gave her permission."

Those words took the breath out of my body but I refused to show it. All of this was happening so fast and my world was spiraling before my eyes.

This was why she had been acting funny, picking fights for no reason, nagging me about new clothes and furniture, and telling me she wanted a half a million-dollar house.

I saw it now. It was never about her wanting more material things. She wanted to get rid of me.

For me to get sick of her constant whining so I would leave her and make room for her baby father to slide back in.

But I must have fucked up her plans by stepping up to the plate and busting my ass to make everything happen.

It all hit me at once and I was ready to hook off on this nigga.

I stepped forward but Jazzmyne jumped between us. "Kendrix, stop! He just got out. He can't get into any altercations or they'll send him back in!" she pleaded.

Her words fell on bewildered ears. She was standing in front of me protecting this nigga like I hadn't just helped raise her son and taken care of her for the past three years. And this nigga was giving her money too? How was all this possible without me knowing?

At that moment I realized I didn't care. This was the worst day of my life but I wasn't about to kill this nigga or this bitch. They could have each other.

I had been played in the worst way, but all I cared about at the moment was Kanai.

"Can I at least say goodbye?" I said, fixing her with what I hoped to be a neutral expression, while on the inside, I was losing it.

Jazzmyne looked from me to Sky, who was still wearing that same stupid smirk, then twisted the dagger.

"We're not sure that's a good idea."

***

The next series of events went like a blur. One minute I was coming home to my family and the next, I was packing bags of my clothes, shoes, and other items.

When it came to the gaming station, at first I was going to take it, but I left it for Kanai. He loved to play and I wouldn't deprive him of that, even though I was sure Sky would probably buy him another one, if he was telling the truth about how he had been providing for Jazzmyne all this time.

Jazzmyne barely even looked at me as I carried the last of my bags out the door and loaded them into my backseat. My trunk was already full.

She stared at me with a pained, but relieved expression. "I'm sorry you found out this way," she offered, and I couldn't even respond.

I scoffed, a million thoughts swirling through my mind, then shook my head and wrenched my car door open, backing out to leave that place for good.

Two streets over, I was about to lose it. I dialed Tremaine and he picked up on the first ring.

"Eyo yo yo!" he said in an excited voice, and I heard Los laughing in the background at the silly way he answered.

"Yo," I let out in a strangled tone. "I need a place to stay for a few."

Tremaine grew serious. "A place to stay? Whatchu mean, nigga? You and wifey fighting?"

"She's not my fucking wife!"

My nostrils flared as I spoke and one tear escaped, but I swiped it away.

Tremaine seemed to immediately catch on that something happened. "Aight nigga, say less. Me and Los will clear out a space. You need help with anything?

I swallowed. "Nah, I'm good. Thanks man. I'll be there in a bit."

I hung up before he responded, then threw my phone in the passenger seat.

Stopping by the liquor store, I bought two fifths of Henny.

After driving aimlessly for a few moments, I entered the highway, then took an exit near a rest stop. While there, I pulled over to the trees and screamed at the top of my lungs, pounding the steering wheel til it cracked.

Then I opened one of the fifths of Henny and took that shit to the face.

After that, everything went black.

Chapter 9: Kyanah

Terrence and I met three years ago. I was twenty five and ashamed to admit he was my first relationship. By that point I had grown kind of desperate because I hadn't had a high school sweetheart like Kaliss and all the other girls my age. In college, I had my head so far in the books that boys didn't gravitate toward me there either.

I didn't sweat it that much though, until after I had graduated college and was a couple years into my career as a human resources officer. All my coworkers were married or in serious relationships, and all of them had kids. I started growing antsy, so I joined a dating site.

Terrance was the first guy I met there. We carried on a few decent conversations before he asked me out on a date. I was nervous to go at first. Although I had been on a few dates before, I was nervous about meeting someone online.

I called my sister Kaliss. She had much more experience with guys. She had high school and college sweethearts and was currently in a serious relationship with her third boyfriend, Rell.

"Just be yourself, Kyanah, and you'll be fine," she said. "Don't have sex with him."

My jaw dropped at her suggestion. I wasn't sure if my sister knew it, but I was still a virgin. "Of course, I'm not going to have sex with him, Kaliss."

"I didn't mean to offend you," she said, "But niggas these days are full of game. If he suggests..."

"I already said I'm not doing anything," I cut her off, offended by the fact that my sister thought I was gullible. Or maybe that wasn't what she thought, but it felt like it at the time.

At the date, Terrance was nice, but he didn't do any of the things I saw in movies or TV shows. He didn't bring me flowers or pull out my chair. He didn't pick me up and hold the car open for me (we met at the restaurant, which was probably safer anyway), and at the end of the meal, we split the check.

In his defense, I offered to pay half, but I was surprised when he agreed. It rubbed me the wrong way, but I rationalized it by saying that I did offer, so why should I blame him for taking me up on it?

When we left the restaurant, he said he didn't want the night to end.

That caused my heart to swell because despite all the minor differences from my expectations, the night had gone well. Terrance was tall, he looked like his pictures, and we had a great conversation.

"How about we chill at my crib and watch a movie?" he suggested.

Immediate red flags raised in my mind, but I pushed them down, reasoning that couples watched movies together all the time.

When we got to his house, he was a perfect gentleman.

His house was also clean and smelled good, but from the looks of it, clearly a man had decorated everything. Sports memorabilia was everywhere and when Terrance gave me a tour, one of his rooms was full of trophies from his time as a star athlete in school. I was impressed by his accomplishments and he made me feel welcome.

He led me back to the living room, offered me a blanket because his living room was kind of chilly, poured me a drink, and allowed me to choose the movie. Halfway through the movie, we were snuggled up under the blanket and my back was pressed up against his chest with our faces next to each other.

I felt him staring at me, then he began trailing kisses down my cheek. My body tingled, and the tingling grew when he got to my neck.

Inhaling a sharp breath, I stopped him, leaning away.

"What?" he said in a husky tone.

I stared at him. "I'm not... ready for all that."

He stared at me with a neutral expression at first, then offered a faint smile. "Oh, you're a good girl, huh?"

I nodded, blushing at the fact that he referred to me that way.

He nodded. "Okay cool. We don't have to do anything that you don't wanna do."

When he said those words, I felt safe and protected. I snuggled up against him again and he didn't try anything else the rest of the night.

But now that he said he wasn't going to try anything, I wished he had.

I'd never been hot in the ass, but as a grown woman, I was curious about sex. There was only so much my fingers could do as far as stimulation. I wanted a man to touch me in the places I'd previously only touched myself.

But there was no way in hell I was telling him that.

***

By our third date, I didn't have to. We had gone out to dinner again and he had paid for the full meal this time. Then we went to his house to watch another movie.

At first I thought he was going to just hold me like he had done last time, but he didn't.

We had barely gotten through the opening credits before he turned to me, his eyes low with a husky expression. "Kyanah," he said, and I loved the way my name sounded on his lips. "You are so beautiful."

I blushed. "Thank you."

His voice lowered another octave. "I'm really enjoying our time together. You're different."

I was elated to hear this because I had already begun envisioning our future together, despite Kaliss' constant warnings to take it slow. I hadn't let on to my sister, but I was falling in love. I thought that because things were going so smoothly, it meant Terrance and I were meant to be together.

"You're different too," I responded, though I didn't have anyone else to compare him to.

His lips curved into a smile, then he gently grabbed my chin and pulled my face to his for a kiss. It was soft and slow at first, then it increased in intensity.

My heart rate also quickened because his lips were smooth and he was a good kisser. The chemistry between us ignited, and before I knew it, we had switched positions and he was on top of me, his hands caressing my body as our lips continued to taste one another.

He gently unbuckled and slid down my skirt and my breath caught in my throat. Terrance pulled back and peered into my eyes.

"I'm a virgin," I blurted, my voice barely above a whisper.

He seemed thrown off by that news at first, then he nodded. "That's cool. I'll take it slow."

I wasn't expecting that as an answer. I thought he would reconfirm with me that I wanted to do this before we did it, but he didn't. He just assumed I wanted to have sex with him and continued sliding my skirt and panties down at once.

Once they were off, I grew nervous. I had never gone this far with a man before. What was I supposed to do?

Terrance eased my legs apart then kissed both my knees, then began trailing kisses down my thighs.

Oh God... My mind grew wild. Was he about to...?

Sucking in a deep breath as his lips touched my center, my eyes popped wide open.

He was about to do what I thought he was.

As his lips and tongue continued to work their magic, I felt myself growing hotter and wetter by the second. Was this really what it felt like?

I didn't have time to think about it because I was already moaning his name. He continued to lick and suck my juices until I felt a growing sensation in the pit of my belly.

Was this an orgasm? Was I about to...?

I never got the chance to find out, because he stopped.

My head popped up at the abrupt departure of his lips and tongue from my slippery folds, but before I could ask what was going on, he was on top of me again, pushing himself inside me.

I yelped in pain as he pushed too hard, but he apologized and eased up.

I wanted to tell him I wasn't ready for that yet, but then another side of my mind said I should have known what was coming. He had just eaten my pussy. What did I expect? He was a grown man and I was a grown woman. It wasn't his fault that I wasn't experienced.

Pretty soon we found a groove and I began to enjoy his gentle thrusts.

Then the thrusts became more forceful and it started hurting again, but before I could tell him to slow down, his body jerked and he quickly pulled out of me, then released himself on my belly.

I stared down at his semen, my mind and body going in different directions, then he said, "I'll be right back," and got off me.

"Where are you..." My voice trailed off as he left the room, then returned with a roll of paper towels. He wiped my belly, then my vagina, then he went to throw the paper towels in the trash.

When he returned, I had already put my skirt and panties back on.

"Hey," he said in a soft voice, and when I looked up at him, he wore a serene expression, like he was completely relaxed.

I didn't know how to feel.

"Did you cum?" he asked.

I didn't respond.

"Kyanah, you good?" he asked after another few moments.

My voice was gravelly as I finally spoke. "I need to... Can I use your bathroom?"

He nodded and I went to his bathroom on wobbly legs, barely making it all the way inside before I dry heaved.

I turned on the sink full blast because I didn't want him to hear me vomiting in his toilet. I didn't want him to get the wrong idea. I didn't want him to think... I didn't even know what I was thinking, much less how he felt.

Bursting into tears, my body let loose whatever emotion it was feeling. There was an emptiness in my heart I couldn't explain.

I kept trying to calm myself down, but the tears kept coming. I felt like I was in that bathroom an hour, but it was only about ten minutes.

Despite that, Terrance didn't come to check on me.

I got myself together and washed my face, then dried it, staring at myself in the mirror and willing a normal expression.

I hoped I hadn't just made the worst mistake of my life by sleeping with him.

When I returned to the living room, he had neatly folded the blanket and was sitting on the couch with his legs crossed at the ankles, texting on his phone.

He looked up at me and chuckled, putting his phone away. "Girl, I almost thought I was going to have to go in there and get you."

I forced a laugh back, then I noticed that the TV was off. Guess movie night was over.

Terrance yawned. "Hey, I gotta work early in the morning. Mind if I take you home?"

I internally blanched at his words but didn't argue. "No, I don't mind," I said in a small voice.

We exited his house and went to his car, and he drove me home.

When I got inside my apartment, I cried again. I didn't know why I was emotional at first, then I realized that part of it was because I lost my virginity after holding it all those years, and the other part was because I kept having the sinking suspicion that something wasn't right about Terrance and me.

I expected to never hear from him again.

But when he called the next day, eager to take me out again, my fears waned. Maybe I had let Kaliss' constant warnings get to my head.

***

It wasn't until two months into our relationship that I noticed a certain female was always hearting and commenting on his pictures on social media.

When I confronted Terrance about it, he laughed off my concerns. "Chill, babe. That's my homegirl, Stephanie."

I narrowed my eyes. "How come you never told me about this so-called homegirl?"

He stared back at me as if I were being unreasonable. "Because she doesn't live around here, but you have nothing to worry about."

I didn't believe him at first, but the following week, I got a random friend request from Stephanie.

I accepted it, thinking it was about to be some drama and she was going to spill the beans about how her and Terrance were together, but that didn't happen.

Instead, a video call came through from her on the messaging app.

I answered, shocked that she was bold enough to call me.

"Hey girl!" she said with a friendly smile.

I studied her. Stephanie was pretty. Brown-skinned with passion twists and a face beat to perfection.

"Hey," I responded, suddenly feeling self-conscious since she was so perfectly put together and I had barely combed my hair that day.

She giggled. "I just wanted to properly introduce myself. Terrance told me you and him had a little disagreement the other day."

I was taken aback once again. Terrance was talking to this woman about me? "Who are you to him?" I asked.

She giggled again. "Girl, that's exactly why I called. Terrance and I are friends. We go way back. But you have nothing to worry about, Kyanah. We're just friends."

The way she said it sounded convincing, but I didn't like the way this whole conversation went down. I was still stuck on the fact that Terrance felt comfortable discussing me with this woman and she felt comfortable calling me to alleviate my feelings like I was some pathetic and insecure little girl who needed her comfort.

"Thank you for clarifying," I said, and Stephanie smiled again.

"No problem at all. Matter of fact, since you and Big Head are so close, how about we chat sometime? I'd love to get to know you."

I was shocked at her suggestion, but I agreed. When we hung up, however, I called Kaliss. After I explained what happened, she said, "Unh uh, sis. I don't like how that all went down. You need to set his ass straight and tell him not to run his mouth about you to no other female."

I agreed with my sister, but I wasn't sure how to approach the topic with Terrance.

I let it go.

A year into our relationship, I got another surprise. I had stopped by to see Terrance on my way home from work and another car was in the driveway.

By this time, we were living together. I had moved in with Terrance at his suggestion a few months prior and things had been smooth between us for the most part.

At first I thought nothing of it, because his friends and family often stopped by, but as I approached the house, the front door opened and Terrance and Stephanie walked out together.

Both of their eyes lit up when they saw me.

My jaw dropped, but before I could recover, Stephanie was throwing her arms around me. "Kyanah, OMG! It's so good to finally meet you in person."

When she pulled back, I stared at her, then at Terrance.

"What are you doing here?" I asked her.

She opened her mouth, but Terrance answered.

"Stephanie just moved back home. Her and that jerk of a boyfriend broke up."

When he said that, I looked back at Stephanie and an indiscernible expression crossed her features before it returned to neutral. "Damn, Big Head. Putting all my business on front street, aren't you?"

I wasn't sure how I felt about Stephanie suddenly moving to town, but I didn't say anything. What was I going to tell her? Go back where she came from? Besides, nothing could happen between them anyway. Terrance loved me and we lived together.

Maybe I should have told her ass to leave, because from that point, things only got worse.

***

Terrance and I were slowly drifting apart and he was spending more and more time with Stephanie. Every time I confronted him about it, he kept saying it was because she was his friend and they had always hung out together before she moved out of town.

I didn't buy it, but when I shared my concerns with Kaliss and she agreed with me, I got scared. Scared that I was losing my man after I had invested so much time into him.

After I had given him my virginity and moved in with him and started to plan our future together.

Kaliss told me I needed to confront Terrance once and for all, but I brushed her off. "I'm probably just overreacting, Kaliss," I said. "They have been friends since childhood."

Kaliss didn't agree, but she didn't push me on it.

Then one day, curiosity got the best of me.

I left work early on Terrance's day off. The idea was to surprise him and then maybe we could go out somewhere to eat then Netflix and chill later on. Once we were relaxed, I could approach him about Stephanie.

But when I arrived at the house, Stephanie's car was outside.

That caused chills to go down my spine because Stephanie worked the same hours as me. She should have been at work.

Letting myself in with my key, it didn't take long to hear moans coming from our bedroom.

My heart dropped along with my purse.

They didn't hear the sound because they were so busy making enough noise to alert the damn neighborhood.

Stephanie was moaning and screaming my man's name and riding him on our freshly purchased bedsheets.

When I entered the bedroom, they were so caught in the throes of passion they didn't notice me.

It was at that moment I felt like a damn fool. Terrance's eyes were closed and his expression was one of pure ecstasy.

He gripped her large breasts as she continued to ride him while he professed his undying love for her over and over.

Terrance had never told me he loved me, even after we moved in together.

I snapped, grabbing a vase from the dresser and stalking over to knock her upside the head with it.

She yelped as I wrenched her off Terrance. "Bitch! I'll kill you!" I grabbed her by the throat as her face reddened with pain and fear, then Terrance realized what was happening and jumped into action, roughly grabbing me off her and throwing me across the room. He threw me so forcefully that I hit my back against the dresser and fell to the floor.

My back filled with pain and I looked up at him, not believing my eyes, but at the same time, finally seeing him for who he was.

"You fucking bastard!" I screamed, but he had the nerve to look at me with disgust.

"You could have killed her!" he said, gesturing at the shattered vase. Then he turned to her and gingerly touched her head, which was bleeding. "Baby, you okay?"

Stephanie's lip trembled. "I want her out of here, Terrance. She knows now; you can erase her from our lives."

Not believing my ears, I shot up to my feet, ready to fight again, but Terrance stood as a barrier between me and his woman. "You take one more step toward us and I'll call the police." He sneered. "Stephanie's right. You know the truth now. I'll pack your things."

The next few moments were hazy.

All I remembered was lunging for them, then being handcuffed by police sometime later.

Now I had an assault charge from Stephanie, a fine, and anger management classes to take, all over someone who lied to me and broke my heart in the process.

Kaliss had bailed me out of jail, but she hit me with another blow on the way home from the precinct.

"Sis, I'm so sorry," she said, and from her voice, I knew there was something she wanted to tell me.

"What is it?" I said in a soft tone.

She stammered as she spoke. "I... I saw them together. A month ago, at a restaurant. It looked like they were on a date. At first I thought they were just out as friends like you said, but then he kissed her."

I turned to her with a numb expression, while she stared ahead at the road, still driving.

"He kissed her?" I repeated in a hollow tone.

She swiped a tear and nodded. "I wanted to tell you, but..."

"Why didn't you?"

Her face crumbled. "Kyanah, you never listened to me about him! Every time I tried to warn you about Terrance, it went in one ear and out the other! I didn't think you'd believe me."

My sister was right in her words - I had ignored all her warnings. But I needed somewhere to direct my anger, so I took it out on her.

"Pull over," I demanded.

Kaliss glanced at me. "What do you mean?"

"Pull over, Kaliss. I won't ride another second beside your disloyal ass."

Her jaw dropped. "Disloyal? I tried to look out for you!"

"Pull the fuck over, before I open this door into traffic!"

Kaliss pulled over and I got out, immediately ordering an Uber.

"Where are you going?" Kaliss asked, looking guilty.

"Don't worry about it," I said, thankful that my ride wasn't far away. When it came, my sister watched me get into the Uber, then we rode off to a hotel. She followed us.

When we got to the hotel, Kaliss tried to approach me again.

"Come on, Kyanah. I..."

"Just get the fuck away from me, Kaliss!" I screeched.

My sister was hurt by the way I treated her, but she had no idea how I felt. She left, and I rented a room for a night.

The next morning, I took another Uber to the storage spot where I had most of my stuff from my previous apartment. I had been meaning to get rid of the stuff, but never got around to it. Good thing I didn't, because now I would need it again. I rented a U-Haul from the storage facility, then headed to Terrance's house to get my car and pack my shit. When I got there, my car was intact, but the locks to the house were changed.

I banged on the door.

Terrance answered with a weary expression. "Kyanah, why are you here?"

My mind reeled at his coldness. "You can't just dismiss me like I don't matter, motherfucker! I'm here to get my shit!"

He didn't budge from his position. "Your bags are packed in the garage."

I blanched at those words, knowing that he and Stephanie probably had their hands all over my shit.

"What about my furniture?"

He looked taken aback. "Your furniture?"

"Yes, nigga." My nostrils flared. "The couch, the new TV, all the shit that I bought into this house."

"Kyanah, don't be petty."

I couldn't believe his audacity. "You're calling me petty while you played in my face for three fucking years?"

He paused. "It wasn't supposed to go down like that."

"Yeah, well who gives a fuck now, right? Move, Terrance, so I can get my things."

With a sigh, he opened the door and I moved all the things I had bought for the house into my waiting U-Haul. I couldn't lift the couch, but Terrance had enough decency to help me get it into the truck.

"We done now?" he asked with attitude, probably pissed that he would now have to buy another replacement. The old one he had before it had stains on it, so I surprised him with a new one after I moved in.

I scoffed, shaking my head. "Yes, we're done. You never have to see my face again."

I drove off, pulling my car behind me with the U-Haul.

I thought I was done with Terrance and Stephanie and ready to pick up the shattered pieces of my heart when I received the summons and learned about the lawsuit.

Now I had to deal with that shit on top of everything else.

***

I sat in my apartment thinking about the situation and couldn't get it out of my mind. Then I heard a knock on my door.

I went to open it and it was Kaliss, holding two bottles of wine. "You ready to forgive me yet?" she asked, holding up the bottles.

I was about to close the door on her, but she stopped me. "Come on, Kyanah, please. I know I should have told you, but I'm sorry. I understand if you don't want to forgive me, but I don't like the idea of you sitting here all by yourself."

When she said those words, they hit me.

I blinked back a tear and walked away from the door, leaving it open for her to come in.

Kaliss closed the door behind her and walked into my apartment, looking around at everything.

"Nice place," she commented, then I broke down.

"Oh, Kyanah!" she said, sitting the bottles on the table and rushing to wrap her arms around me.

Chapter 10: Kendrix

I trudged up the three flights of stairs to the apartment I shared with Tremaine and Los. As soon as I opened the door into the hallway from the stairwell, my nostrils caught the pungent scent of marijuana.

I was no stranger to Mary Jane, but at the same time I wasn't much of a smoker. I did it from time to time with Los and Tremaine, but I hadn't smoked in months prior to my breakup with Jazzmyne. Now the scent was making me sick to my stomach.

I prayed the smell wasn't coming from Tremaine and Los' apartment as I approached number 412, but of course, it was.

A waft of smoke blasted me as soon as I opened the door, giving me an instant headache.

"Damn, niggas! Open a window or something," I said, then grew more irritable when I saw that they were in the middle of a card game with both of their girls. Well, Los had a girlfriend, Tracey, but Tremaine was entertaining one of his jumpoffs.

"Hey, Kendrix," Tracey greeted.

"Hey," I responded, lightening up my mood as Tremaine opened a window as I requested.

"You want in on the next game?" Los offered. "We ordered pizza and wings too."

I shook my head, holding up my bag of KFC. "I'm good, I already got something on the way home."

Tremaine stared at my bag, then snickered, reaching over to nudge Los before returning to his seat. "That nigga stuck on chicken ever since Kyanah."

Los looked at me and burst out laughing.

"Fuck y'all niggas," I said, my shoulders tensed. "Nobody's thinking about Kyanah."

Los chuckled again. "Yeah, okay. If you ask me, you should go down there and get her number already. It's clear y'all had chemistry."

Tracey and the other girl were staring between me, Tremaine, and Los like we were giving them some juicy gossip.

"Kendrix, let me find out you done moved on already. Tread lightly though, babe. I still owe your ex an ass whooping!"

"Tracey!" Los hissed, trying to shut his girlfriend up, but the cat was out of the bag already. Apparently, I had been the subject of one of their pillow talk discussions.

Los gave me a guilty smile but I shrugged it off, opening my bag of chicken.

Tremaine's jumpoff didn't seem to get the memo that the conversation wasn't wanted. She looked between Los and Tracey. "What did his ex do?"

Tremaine stopped her and I was glad he did because I wasn't about to sit there and pour out my relationship saga for some thirsty female to hear. "Girl, stop being nosey and get back to the game!" He began snatching up the cards. "And I gotta deal again, 'cause I got a feeling one of y'all niggas cheated when I went to open the window."

Los immediately started complaining as he tossed his hand at Tremaine. "Whatever nigga. You're only saying that 'cause y'all was losing!"

Tremaine reshuffled the deck and began dealing once again.

I was grateful for the distraction, and pretty soon I was zoned out, catching a contact from their smoke. As I ate my chicken and half-tuned into their game, however, an emptiness filled my heart.

I didn't know if it was the marijuana, my recent breakup, Tremaine and Los' comments, or the fact that they were sitting around the table with their women having fun, but a strong sense of loneliness enveloped me. It was so strong I felt like it would swallow me whole.

"I'm-a get some air," I announced as I abruptly stood, then exited the apartment. Stumbling down the stairs, I made it outside, my emotions hitting me the moment I tasted the fresh air and stared into the darkening sky.

I was a good man to Jazzmyne and she fucked me up by what she did.

Try as I might, I couldn't shake the pain.

I stared back at the building, wishing I had somewhere else to go. With Tracey and Tremaine's jumpoff at the apartment, I felt like a fifth wheel.

At the same time, it wasn't like I could kick them out. It wasn't my apartment.

Clicking my key fob, I walked over to my car and climbed into the driver's seat.

Pulling out my phone, I began my apartment search. I had been lingering at Tremaine and Los' apartment partially out of depression and partially because I enjoyed spending time with my boys, but the past few weeks I started feeling trapped, like I needed to make a move.

Time to start over.

Chapter 11: Kyanah

I just finished my first anger management session and all it did was reignite my fury at Stephanie and Terrance.

I had to sit through twelve weeks of this bullshit, with somebody explaining to me how to express myself instead of resorting to violence.

It wouldn't be so bad if I needed it. I didn't need anger management, I needed to knock that bitch's head off her shoulders.

Rightfully, my anger should have been solely directed at Terrance, and the majority of it was, but I couldn't get over the fact that Stephanie had played in my face right along with him.

Wasn't there some type of girl code?

How could she feel comfortable fucking him in our bed knowing he had a whole girlfriend living with him?

I couldn't get over the shit so along with the anger management, I signed up for kickboxing classes in the same building.

That would be a better way to blow off my steam. Once I hit the bag a few times, I would feel better.

Maybe it would help me get in shape too, which I needed after all the comfort meals I had been eating.

Walking down the stairs from the third floor of the community building, I could not wait to get to the gym.

I had a membership at another gym before my breakup with Terrance, but since he and Stephanie had a restraining order on me and I never wanted to see either of their faces again, I canceled that membership and took one out at Community Fitness. I was glad I did too because they offered all kinds of classes, including the one I was taking tonight.

My anger at Stephanie and Terrance began to subside as I entered the locker room to change into some leggings, sneakers, and a loose-fitting t-shirt, then threw my curls up into a ponytail. I also took out my earrings and locked them in my locker, along with my cell phone.

By the time I exited the locker room and entered the room where the kickboxing class would be held, my mood had transformed.

Gone as my anger, replaced with excitement.

I smiled as two other girls stopped their stretching to greet me.

"Hey!" one of them said. "First day, huh?"

I nodded with a shy smile. I was always nervous meeting new people. "Is the class hard?"

One of them shrugged. "It's a challenge, but you will definitely enjoy it."

"Plus it doesn't hurt that our teacher is fine as hell!" the other said, and they shared a giggle.

That threw me for a loop. Since it was a women's kickboxing class, I assumed the teacher would be a woman, but from the looks on their faces as the teacher entered the room, I encountered a second surprise. Our teacher was *him*.

When we caught eyes, I couldn't help but to glance at his bulging muscles before returning my gaze to his face.

He smirked but didn't say anything about me checking him out. "Kyanah," he said instead. "Are you lost? I'm surprised you would join my class."

The other women were staring at our interaction with mischievous grins. "Kendrix, you two know each other?" the first woman said, gesturing between me and our teacher.

It was at that moment that I realized it had been over two months of me seeing and speaking to this man randomly in our building and I was just now learning his name.

Kendrix smiled and before I could answer, he said, "We're neighbors."

I felt awkward as hell signing up for his class without knowing it. Part of me wanted to leave, but before I could make a move toward the door, a few other women walked in and Kendrix's expression turned serious. "Alright, ladies! Let's get started with our warmup. Bianca and Alena, how about y'all show Kyanah the ropes?"

Since he didn't seem like he was going to be an asshole toward me, I stayed.

I was glad I did.

It was a challenge, like Bianca and Alena said, but I couldn't deny that Kendrix was a good teacher.

Even when I kept messing up on the footwork he had us doing, he was patient with me until I got the movements.

"That's right, Kyanah!" He said, when I had done a successful round of Karaoke's without tripping over my feet in the process. He fist-bumped me and I gave him a genuine smile.

"I can't believe I did it!" I exclaimed. "I didn't think I was gonna catch it on my first night."

"All it takes is patience and practice," he said, and the look in his eyes stilled my heart for a moment. It was as if he was speaking about more than the Karaoke drill. Like he was sending me a deeper message about life in general.

My face flushed and he winked, then focused on the other girls while I recovered.

By the end of the night, I was drenched in sweat and exhausted in my body, but my mind felt clearer.

I was humming as I entered the locker room with the other girls.

My happy mood continued on the way home.

When I pulled in the parking lot, I halfway expected to meet Kendrix there and thought maybe we might enter the building together.

But as I scanned the lot, I saw that his car was already parked, which meant he made it in before me.

"Chill, Kyanah, he's not the focus anyway," I whispered.

Chapter 12: Kendrix

I had been teaching the women's kickboxing class for five years and never once did I see Kyanah in the building. Granted, it was a whole community center. There was a gym, meeting rooms, a spa, gift shop, and a number of other types of businesses, but it surprised the hell out of me to walk in and see her there.

At first I thought she would give me attitude, but instead she looked nervous, like my presence had thrown her off as much as hers did me.

Thankfully, we were able to get through the session without issue and I got to see another side of her.

She wasn't as bitter as I thought she was.

When she finally cracked a smile after she got the Karaoke's right, it warmed something deep within my soul.

I didn't know what it was about her, but seeing Kyanah's smile made me want it to make it happen again. Something told me she hadn't smiled like that in a while. At least she hadn't any other time I had seen her.

By the time she left, it was like the perpetual chip on her shoulder had lifted, but I was no fool. Anybody would feel good after a great workout, especially if you nailed a move you were trying to learn.

Our next interaction would tell me more, if she returned to the class.

I was already looking forward to seeing her again, though I didn't know why.

I had repeatedly told Tremaine and Los I didn't want Kyanah, despite their constant urging for me to ask for her number.

I laughed it off and accused them of only wanting more of her chicken, yet every time I saw her, I felt drawn to her like a magnet.

It scared the shit out of me.

It was way too soon for me to be catching feelings for another woman. It had been a little over two months since Jazzmyne and I broke up, and Kyanah and I started off on the wrong foot.

I needed to get my shit together and find another apartment, not try to push up on some other woman.

One of the places I filled out the application for left me a voicemail.

Maybe a few months after I moved into my own place, I would think about trying to find another woman. It wasn't time now.

But as I showered, I kept seeing Kyanah's smile flashing through my mind.

As I laid in bed that night, I imagined her next to me, wondering what she would feel like snuggled up against my body.

That curly hair, splayed all over her head. Those chinky eyes, staring at me like she wanted me.

Now I knew I was fantasizing.

Never in any of our interactions did Kyanah give me the remote feeling that she was into me. She blushed a few times, sure, but she made it clear she was off limits.

I should be off limits too because I damn sure wasn't interested in jumping back into a relationship with another woman.

Drifting off to sleep, my mind finally rested from my swirling thoughts.

Chapter 13: Kyanah

I stared at the big ass box before me, fuming that the delivery company had not followed my directions.

I had ordered a new bookcase for my apartment and explicitly told them to bring the box to my apartment door. Apparently, when I said that, they must have taken it as me wanting them to leave it at the security door, which meant that now I had to find a way to lug this heavy ass box down the stairs and down the hallway to my apartment.

I had just gotten home from work. I was excited when I saw the notification during my lunch break that it had been delivered, but my smile erased when I noticed in the picture that the delivery driver had taken that he had left it outside the security door.

Sucking my teeth, I formulated a plan. Maybe I could catty-corner this shit through the security door. Getting it to the stairwell and down the stairs wouldn't be too much of a problem, but there was a long ass hallway that led to my apartment, which was at the end of the hall near the back door of the building.

I shook my head, then fought with the security door to get it unlocked and opened. That was another issue in itself. I had complained to the landlord about the security door when I first moved in, and they assured me they would be getting it fixed soon so it would be easier to unlock.

Thank God I was never chased by a stalker on my way into the building, because my ass would have been caught.

I wrangled the lock open, then propped the security door open with my leg while reaching for the box with my arms.

I should have pushed it closer to the door before opening it. Now I couldn't get a good grip. Sucking my teeth, I grasped the box as hard as I could and pulled it toward me, but the seventy-pound bookcase proved to be difficult to move.

Movement outside the glass pane next to the outer door caught my eye.

As if fate had forced our paths to cross, Kendrix was jogging up the steps.

When he opened the outer door, we caught eyes.

"What's up, Kyanah? You need help with that?"

Before I could answer, he was lifting the long rectangular box with ease and hoisting it up on his shoulder.

"What you got in here?" he asked.

Since he was helping me, plus we seemed to be in a better place after the kickboxing class, I didn't give him an attitude. "It's a bookcase."

He nodded, then I held the security door open wider to let him through. I watched his well-built back, re-envisioning what he looked like the other night in that black tank top as he carefully walked toward the short flight of stairs, then turned the corner toward my apartment.

Snapping out of my lustful thoughts, I scampered down the stairs after him and walked behind him until he got to my door. When we got there, I maneuvered around him and unlocked my door, pushing it wide open. Kendrix walked inside first, looking over his shoulder at me. "Where do you want this? In the living room?"

I nodded and swallowed back a smile. I didn't know why I felt all giddy inside. All he did was carry a damn box. It was common courtesy. *But it also shows that he's a gentleman,* my mind reasoned.

Kendrix laid the box down then turned toward me. "You need help putting it together, or you good?"

"I'm good," I quickly said, before he could get any more ideas about helping me. His presence in my apartment was enough to make my heart involuntarily flutter. "I actually like putting furniture together," I added, to let him know I wasn't trying to brush him off.

He nodded. "My mom does the same thing."

A brief silence filled the room with those words. I reminded him of his mom?

That was an interesting comment, but I refused to look too deeply into it.

Kendrix nodded again and walked past me toward the door. "Let me know if you need anything else," he said, before he exited my apartment.

Tongue-tied, I couldn't do anything but watch him as I approached the open door and saw him walking down the hall.

"Thank you," I called out, and he turned and waved before entering the stairwell.

When I closed the door to my apartment, I fought back another smile.

Chapter 14: Kendrix

Kyanah was polite when I helped her with the box a few days ago, but I got the feeling that she wanted me to hurry up and leave her apartment once I brought it inside.

I didn't feel any type of way about it since it wasn't like we were friends or anything. We only saw each other in passing, despite living in the same building.

At the same time, as the night of the next kickboxing class drew closer, I couldn't help but hope she would show up again.

I got there a few minutes early, straightening up the room to take my mind off my desire to see her.

When students started entering, however, she wasn't among them.

My hope faltered when it was time for class to start and she hadn't arrived.

Shaking off my disappointment, I focused on my other students. We were here for a class, not a love connection.

"Alright ladies," I announced. "Let's get ready for..." My voice trailed off as Kyanah burst into the room, wearing a pair of skintight leggings and a sports bra.

"Damn," I muttered under my breath, and tried to tear my eyes away to keep from ogling her as she took her position amongst the other girls.

I refocused, but she caught me eyeing her before I did.

To my elation, she gave me another smile.

I clapped my hands to get the warmup started.

Pretty soon, the class was underway. We started with light stretching, then transitioned to footwork.

"Remember ladies, it's all about speed and agility!" I called out as they each skipped back and forth across the wide room, then did Karaoke's.

After that it was time for weighted Goblet squats, which they often hated, but I encouraged for strength and balance.

"This is only gonna help your core," I said, when they moved to forearm planks, then it was time for everyone's favorite part: beating the shit out of the bags.

I always got a kick out of the mean expressions on women's faces as they kicked and punched the heavy bags. It was like they were each envisioning an enemy or ex-boyfriend and knocking their head between the washer and dryer.

I encouraged each of the ladies to go hard but keep their form.

That was when I noticed that Kyanah seemed to be faltering.

She wasn't hitting the bag as hard as she had last class.

I stepped over to her while keeping an eye on the other girls. "You good?" I asked, my voice full of concern.

She swallowed and nodded, but from her facial expression it was clear she wasn't okay. My mind drifted to how she had come to class late and I wondered if something had happened on her way there.

"Come on girl, you got this," I encouraged, and told her to kick the bag harder.

She lifted her leg and kicked, but the bag barely moved.

"Come on Kyanah, kick that motherfucker's ass!"

That caused the other ladies to burst into laughter, and Kyanah's expression morphed into a look of fury before she leaned back and kicked the bag as hard as she could, but unfortunately, she underestimated her distance from the bag and hit it with her shin.

Her face immediately crumbled in pain and I reached out to catch her before she fell.

"My bad, that was my fault," I said, gently rubbing her leg after I eased her to the floor.

The other girls crowded around. "Want me to get some ice?" Alena asked, and Kyanah and I nodded simultaneously. Her and Bianca ran off to grab some.

"Thanks," Kyanah said, when they returned.

We wrapped Kyanah's shin and situated her in a corner while she soothed her leg, but as the class wore on, I felt terrible about what happened. If I hadn't been screaming in her ear, she never would have hurt herself.

By the time class ended, Kyanah had returned, but she was still punching and kicking the bag lightly as if she didn't have much strength.

The other ladies slapped high fives with each other and exited the room, but I called Kyanah back.

Her eyes widened when I called her name and she approached me as if she was nervous.

"What is it?" she asked, wiping her forehead with a hand towel.

I studied her. "How's your leg feeling?"

She shrugged but looked at the ground. "It's fine. It doesn't hurt anymore."

"You sure?"

She nodded, then inched up her legging to show me. There was a bruise where she had hurt herself. I gently rubbed it. "You sure you don't want to get it checked out?"

She shook her head, then slid her legging back down. "I'm fine. I bruise easily anyway."

A faraway look crossed her eyes before she stared at me again.

"I noticed you didn't want to beat the bag today," I joked. "What's up? You got all your anger out last class?"

She shook her head, but then her eyes grew glassy like I had said something wrong.

I felt like an asshole. "My bad, I didn't mean to offend you."

She shook her head again. "It's fine... Just going through a lot right now."

"Wanna talk about it?"

She swallowed. "Nope. I'll be okay."

She looked so sad I wanted to reach out and hold her but that would be wildly inappropriate and would probably turn her off.

At the same time, I sensed she needed a friend.

"I know we don't know each other well, but whatever it is you will get through it."

She stared blankly as if she hadn't heard me at first, then she approached the bag.

I opened my mouth to ask her what she was doing, but she reared back and punched it hard as fuck. If she wasn't still wearing her protective gloves she would have broken her hand.

I watched as she struck the bag with her other fist, then leaned back to kick it, this time with precision.

I quickly got into position, sensing she needed to let some shit loose.

"That's it, watch your form," I said, as a look of determination crossed her eyes.

Kyanah struck the bag again and again. At first she started slow, practicing the moves from the class, then she switched to a street style and started raining blows on the bag like she was beating somebody's ass.

I wanted to stop her but didn't.

She kept beating the bag until tears poured from her eyes. Then she stepped back with a pained expression before collapsing onto the floor in a fit of sobs.

I had no idea what just happened, but I found myself kneeling on the floor next to her, then grabbing her in my arms.

I held her for a long time, and neither of us said a word, but I had a feeling she had just reached a breakthrough in whatever situation she was dealing with.

Chapter 15: Kyanah

The moment I shared with Kendrix after our class touched my heart in indescribable ways. Despite how mean I had been to him over the past couple months, when Kendrix saw that I was feeling vulnerable, instead of ridiculing me, he stepped in to help.

I also couldn't get over the gentle way he held me when he caught my fall, and how he was careful as he wrapped my leg with the ice, then made sure I felt better afterward.

Kendrix was a good man, I was just a broken woman.

I had never felt so lost in my life. I went back and forth from feeling worthless and stupid to recognizing that what I had gone through wasn't uncommon. Plenty of women got played every day. Most found a way to move on with their lives afterward, but I was stuck.

I needed to shake up my routine, so I decided to visit a church I always drove by on my way home from work. The service started at eleven, and I pulled up right on time.

As I approached the building, I caught a familiar frame as he led an older woman into the building.

"Kendrix?" I called out, and he turned to face me. His brows scrunched in confusion at first, then he broke into a welcoming smile.

"Kyanah? What are you doing here?"

The woman he was walking with had reached the top of the steps and she turned around too. From one look at her, I knew she was his mother. She was a beautiful woman, darker skinned just like Kendrix, and she was wearing a white and gold skirt-suit with a matching hat, heels, and purse. Seeing her all decked out and Kendrix looking dapper in his dress shirt and tie with grey suit pants made me smile. "Is this your mother?" I asked.

"Yes I am," the woman answered and extended her hand for me to take it. The corners of her eyes crinkled as she smiled. I carefully walked up the steps to approach her and shake her hand. "Kyanah, is it?" she said.

"Yes, ma'am," I said, while Kendrix continued to study me from the corner of my eye.

"How do you and my son know each other?" she asked.

"We live in the same building," I answered.

Just then, another older woman appeared at the front door. "Beverly, what's taking you so long?" When she saw me talking to Kendrix's mother, her eyes lit up, then she gave a knowing smile. "Oh, I'll leave you all to it."

"To what?" I wanted to ask but didn't dare.

Beverly winked at me. "I hope you enjoy the service, honey."

"I'm sure I will."

We entered the building with Kendrix holding the door for us.

I eyed him as I walked past him and he licked his lips and continued staring at me.

My breath caught in my throat and sinful thoughts of him flooded my mind but I pushed them away. We headed inside the sanctuary and Kendrix followed his mother at first, but she turned and shooed him away. "You go sit with your friend," she said, and gave me a wink.

Kendrix turned to me when she walked away. "You cool with us sitting together?" He looked nervous all of a sudden.

I shrugged. "I don't bite."

Chapter 16: Kendrix

The reason I asked if Kyanah minded me sitting with her was because I wasn't sure I could handle the temptation. We were in the house of the Lord, but the way she was wearing that curvy pink dress had my mind in other places.

My mother seemed to like her, which was a good thing, but at the same time, I didn't want her hastily putting the two of us together. Kyanah and I had just barely gotten on good terms.

Ma turned back and smiled at me, then continued her conversation in the second row with Mother Theresa and Mother Sue. I knew they were gossiping about me, probably planning me and Kyanah's wedding.

I wasn't going to worry about it. I turned to Kyanah and spoke in a low voice.

"Have you visited here before?"

She turned and looked at me, and the softness of her eyes caused my dick to jump. See, this was why us sitting next to each other was a bad idea. I discreetly grabbed a hymn book and played off my growing erection by laying it open across my lap. Then I focused on her answer.

She shook her head. "No, this is my first time, but I always pass it on the way home from work.

"What do you do for work?" I asked, suddenly curious to know everything there was to know about her.

She pushed a curly strand behind her ear. "I work as a human resources manager for a tech company."

I nodded. "That's dope. I'm a forklift driver."

She looked me up and down. "Always working with your hands, huh?"

I cracked a grin. "You haven't seen the half of what I can do."

Her face flushed and I regretted the inappropriate comment, then cleared my throat and faced forward.

Pretty soon, the service was starting. The praise team came forward and started singing, and I was pleasantly surprised to see Kyanah get up and clap her hands, singing along to the song.

I got up too.

Then came time for prayer, and they asked everyone to hold hands with those in their pew. I clasped Kyanah's hand and intertwined my fingers with hers. Her hands were soft and warm, just like I imagined the rest of her body to be.

As the service wore on, I was supposed to be paying attention, but I couldn't help sneaking glances at Kyanah.

A couple times, I caught her glancing my way too.

Chapter 17: Kyanah

The next few weeks were smooth. It seemed that attending Kendrix's church was what I needed to get my mind moving in the right direction. Ironically, the pastor's sermon the day I attended was titled, "Letting Go and Moving On," and it touched my heart as he spoke about how pain could consume us if we let it. I didn't want pain to consume me. What had happened between me, Terrance, and Stephanie was over. They had moved on and I needed to do the same, no matter how bad they had done me.

I was getting the hang of the kickboxing thing. Continuing with Kendrix's class was another good decision I'd made. He was an excellent teacher and the other girls in the class were cool. My hunch was right that kickboxing would help me get over my anger more than that irritating ass anger management class. It wasn't that the leader or group was bad, it was that the reason I was there was because of what Stephanie and Terrance had done to me. I had to be punished, while they moved on into a life of bliss.

As the next few weeks wore on, I found myself thinking of Stephanie and Terrance less and less, but Kendrix more.

I couldn't help but be attracted to him and something told me he was feeling me too.

But it was too soon to be trying to jump into a relationship with another man while I was still fulfilling my legal obligations from the last relationship.

Maybe my ass needed a therapist instead of anger management.

Or maybe, the naughty side of my mind said as I stared at Kendrix's print while he stood in front of our class, *maybe you need some dick.*

We had already completed our warmup and Kendrix was gesturing as he introduced us to a new combination that we needed to learn for the bag. I loved to watch him as he explained things because you could tell he was serious about what he was doing. A man with passion. I wondered if it translated to the bedroom.

He looked at me right as I had that thought and my face reddened because I knew he caught me staring at his bulge.

I quickly refocused, but he had to know someone would look with those gray sweatpants he was wearing.

Kendrix smirked, then focused on the class.

"Alright, who wants to be first up to demonstrate the new move?"

Alena volunteered and I watched her as Kendrix held the bag while she completed the move. It was a combination of jabs and kicks that would probably take me a few tries before I grasped it.

My eye-hand coordination wasn't the best, but no one from the class ever got on me about it.

"Everyone has strengths and weaknesses," Kendrix had said with a shrug when I complained about it in one class. "You just gotta stay patient and keep practicing. You got this. You've come a long way in just a few short weeks."

Those words made me feel empowered.

Kendrix always seemed to have that effect on me.

The more time I spent with him, though our sessions were brief, the more I got to see that my first impression of him was wrong.

I was so caught up in being angry at my breakup that I hadn't realized Kendrix was a good guy.

He would make a woman happy one day, if he wasn't doing that already.

A pang of jealousy swept through me at the thought of Kendrix with another woman, but I pushed it back. He wasn't my man, and I had just finished reminding myself that it was too soon for me to embark on another relationship.

But as tonight's class wore on, I couldn't help but to keep staring at his bulge and wondering if it was as big as it looked and if he knew how to work it.

That was one thing that always bothered me about Terrance. He was average size, not that I had anything to compare it to, but that wasn't the problem. The problem was that the majority of the time when we had sex, he finished before I had a chance to cum.

When he rolled over and dozed off, I would be left to my own devices to get my orgasm.

I wanted Kendrix to give me an orgasm...

He called my name just as I had that thought, shaking me from my lustful thoughts.

"Kyanah, you're up!"

My eyes widened as I stood to demonstrate the move. Kendrix wanted each of us to do it once before the class to get our form right before he let us break off in pairs to use the bags.

Surprisingly, I got the combination right the first time.

"That's what I'm talking about!" he said, and I grinned and went back to my seat.

Kendrix showed us a couple more new moves before the night was over, then it was time to head home.

I opted to take my shower at the gym because I didn't want to funk up my car on the way home.

When I emerged, the building was empty except for maintenance, like usual.

I grabbed some takeout on the way home and when I pulled into the parking lot, I saw that Kendrix had already arrived.

Ever since I learned which car was his, I always found myself looking out for him when I pulled into the lot.

I entered the building and headed to my apartment, opening my bag of food, then heading to the cabinet to grab a plate.

When I grabbed the plate, I heard a light knock at my door.

Whipping my head around, I wondered who it was? Kaliss wouldn't come over this late without calling first.

I approached the door with caution, thankful that I always slid my chain when I entered the apartment.

"Who is it?" I called out.

"It's me," Kendrix's voice could be heard on the other side of the door.

I was surprised he would come to my apartment out of the blue, but that didn't stop me from opening the door.

"Hey." I greeted him with an involuntary smile. "What are you doing here?"

He licked his lips and looked nervous. My eyes trailed downward and I noticed that he was wearing a different outfit from the one he wore in class, and he smelled like he had freshly showered.

"Can I come in for a second?" he asked.

I eyed him, then opened the door wider for him to enter, closing it behind me.

When we entered the living room/dining area, he noticed my bag of food. "Oh, my bad. Did I interrupt your meal?"

I let out a nervous giggle. "Kind of, but you're good. What's going on?"

He looked me up and down before he explained the reason for his visit. "I just wanted to share with you that I finally found an apartment. I'm moving out tomorrow."

I was taken aback by this news.

"Found an apartment?" I repeated, stammering over my words as a sense of sadness swept over me. I hadn't known he was looking for a new apartment.

He seemed to sense my confusion. "Oh, that's right, I never explained. I was only living here temporarily. Tremaine and Los let me crash for a few when I..." His voice trailed off. "While I got my shit together," he finished.

I still wasn't following, but I wasn't about to bombard him with questions. It wasn't my business, though I was flattered by the fact that he felt the need to tell me.

"Well congratulations on your new place," I said, forcing a smile. "We'll miss you around here."

He smirked and licked his lips at those words. "I bet you will," he joked. "You won't have anybody to carry those heavy ass boxes for you anymore."

I giggled but waved him off. "I'm sure Tremaine and Los would help, for some chicken."

He chuckled and took a step closer to me. "But they can't do it like me."

His tone and facial expression told me he was no longer talking about boxes, but I wasn't ready to go there with him.

I swallowed. "I bet your woman will let you help with her boxes. Or your mom," I added as an afterthought, as he took another step toward me and heat swept through my body.

Now he was up on me and it made me feel like it did the first night we met, when we stood toe to toe in my kitchenette and I was captivated by his height and masculine scent.

"I don't have a woman," he said softly. "Though I wouldn't mind getting to know you better."

My eyes bulged at those words. He was putting me on the spot. All this time, we had been lightly flirting with one another, sharing glances and comments, but neither one of us had come out and said anything about catching feelings.

"I got a crush on you, girl," he drawled, staring down into my eyes as if he had heard my thoughts.

I peered up at him. "A crush on me? That's surprising." Then I looked down at the floor.

He lifted my chin. "It shouldn't be. You're beautiful." Then his eyes switched from seduction to concern. "You know that, right?"

I nodded. "I do, but I've been through some situations that have thrown me for a loop, is all."

"Yeah?"

I nodded again.

"Well whoever that nigga is, he was a damn fool. But how about you let me take your mind off him?"

Before I could ask what he meant by that, his lips were on mine. The moment was so electric, I pulled back in shock, gasping at his sudden movement.

Kendrix smirked and pulled me close, kissing me again. This time, I sank into him. He felt so good, and the way his strong arms enveloped me felt like heaven.

Then I had a flashback of the last time I let a nigga get this close and pushed away from him. "I-we shouldn't do this," I stammered. "This is nothing but pheromones-I mean, endorphins."

Kendrix cracked another grin. "Pheromones, huh? You saying you wanna fuck me?"

What the hell was wrong with this man? The way he was coming on to me was making me hot as hell. All types of feelings were reawakening that I thought I would never feel again.

I couldn't help but to glance downward at his bulge before answering. "You got a potty mouth," I joked. "It was a slip of the tongue."

"How about we slip our tongues together again?" Kendrix responded, undeterred by my half-hearted attempt at rejecting him.

I stared at his crotch one more time before I leveled him with a gaze. "Boy please. You don't even look like you can fuck. You're a good fighter, I'll give you that, but that hand and eye coordination may not translate to the bedroom."

Kendrix eyed me like I had just issued a challenge. "You wanna bet?" He pulled me toward him again.

I pushed against his chest, but my efforts were weak as I felt how firm and muscular it was.

"Come on, Kyanah," Kendrix murmured. "Stop acting like you don't want me."

"I don't want you," I lied, but he chuckled.

"Yeah? Then prove it."

Before I knew it, he had cupped the back of my head and was kissing me again. It felt so intimate, so forceful, yet gentle, I almost swooned.

Not to be outdone, I grabbed his dick through his basketball shorts and stroked it.

Why did I do that? My pussy started leaking when I felt how thick it was. I wanted him, bad, and the fact that he knew I wanted him only turned me on more. Fleeting thoughts filled my mind, telling me we were moving too fast, but I ignored them.

Kendrix broke our kiss. "Don't put your hands on me like that unless you want to take it there."

"Take it where?" I said in a low voice.

His gaze pierced mine as he answered. "To ecstasy."

My breath hitched, because it had been far too long, but the sensible side of me tried to hold back. "You probably couldn't turn me on if you tried."

"Your nipples are telling a different story." He licked his lips and suddenly, I wanted them on my nipples. "Whatever, that don't mean shit," I said, and moved to push his head but he grabbed my hand and gently kissed my forearm, then licked it, causing my pussy to cream a little more. I wanted that tongue to touch other places now.

Kendrix began kissing me again, this time with more passion. I grew weak in the knees. My lady parts were pulsating. If we didn't stop now, I was gonna fuck him.

At the same time, why fight the feeling? *Does this make me a whore?* I was calculating how long me and Kendrix had known each other when he pulled back again.

"Say the word, Kyanah. Tell me you want me to bring you to ecstasy."

My face reddened. I was taken aback by his slick talk but couldn't deny I liked it.

He kissed me again. "Tell me."

"I ain't telling you…" My voice trailed off as he swept me off my feet and carried me to my bedroom. My body was trembling. My mind said I didn't want this, but my body said, *hell yes I do*.

The moment Kendrix laid me down and I felt his body weight on top of me, I knew it was on. The feel of him on top of me made me moan by itself.

Kendrix smiled, then he grabbed my hand, leading it to his dick, which was standing at attention underneath his basketball shorts. "See what you do to me?" he asked.

I blushed.

Then his finger slid inside my shorts. "Don't tell me I got you hot and heated already. I ain't even got started yet," he commented as his fingers traced the length of my clit. I bit my lower lip, then pulled his head down for another kiss.

He continued, then went to my neck. The way his tongue swirled around was driving me crazy. "Kendrix!" I screamed, but that only made him go harder.

When he left me breathless, he started on the other side and I couldn't take it anymore. Legs wide open, I enveloped him and began grinding against him and moaning while he flickered his tongue across my neck. "Kendrix," I said, breathless again, and he pulled back and stared down his long lashes at my face.

He continued to mesmerize me with those honey brown eyes, our breathing growing in sync, then a guilty expression crossed his features and he stopped. "Hey... I don't want to push you into anything you don't want," he said.

My body grew hot and cold.

Now that he had me all hot and bothered, he was getting cold feet? What did he mean, he didn't want to push me? "I do want it," I urged, ready for him to fill me up.

He was still reluctant. "You sure? I don't want to take advantage of you, Kyanah."

His sudden show of concern was starting to irritate me. "It's a little late for that, isn't it?"

Those words stopped him cold. "I'm sorry," he said, and was about to get up but I grabbed his arms. "Where are you going?"

"I'm not about to take advantage of you."

"You're not," I said. "Why do you keep saying that?" Frustration was building the more I felt his weight pressing down on me but he wasn't trying to give me what I wanted.

He swallowed. "That night a couple weeks ago. Why were you crying?"

Why would he bring that up now? Clearly, this wasn't the right moment!

"Kendrix, I don't want to talk about that," I said, fighting to keep my tone calm and expression neutral.

He still seemed uneasy. "It seemed like you were really upset."

"Why are you thinking about that now? Right when we're about to have sex."

He swallowed and shook his head. "I'm sorry."

"You don't have to be sorry. We can talk about that later. Right now, let's get back to what we were doing."

He shook his head. "No, I should have known better. You're in a vulnerable state. I shouldn't have pushed up on you like I did. I'm sorry."

He moved to get up again, but I held his arms. "Did you mean it?"

"Huh?"

I spoke in a firmer tone. "Did you mean it?" I repeated. "When you said you liked me. That you wanted me. You said it like you wanted this to go further than tonight."

He stared at me like he was offended. "Of course I meant it. I'm not some fuck-boy."

"Alright then, let's do it."

I didn't know why I expected him to keep going. He didn't.

Kendrix stared at me for a long time, then he gently pressed his lips against mine before pulling back. "When we take it there, I want it to be right," he said.

That calmed me down, though I was still slightly pissed. He got up off me, and my body immediately felt cold and lonely where just a few moments ago, it was hot and horny.

"Kendrix, you don't have to leave."

He stared at me. "Trust me, I'm not leaving in the way you think. I want you, Kyanah. I meant what I said. But we gotta do this shit right, or we might as well not do it at all."

Those words hit me and I finally snapped out of my lust filled haze.

I swallowed in shame. "Okay," I said in a small voice.

He gently grabbed my hand and intertwined our fingers. It was a small gesture, but it felt so right.

I stared at our hands, then looked back up at him.

"Take my number down," he urged. "I'm gonna text you when I get settled into my apartment."

Chapter 18: Kendrix

I was kicking myself the whole next day about what I had almost done to Kyanah. Not that I didn't want her sexually, but at the same time, I knew better.

She had just opened up to me recently, and I was already trying to dig into her draws.

Then the fact that I was trying to fuck her before we even went on a date or I got her number rubbed me the wrong way. Kyanah was a good woman. She deserved to be treated like a queen. And I intended to be her king, if she would still have me after last night's debacle.

Along with feeling bad for almost taking advantage of her, I also felt like a simp for getting her all hot and bothered just to let her down. I felt like a chump, though in my heart I sensed it was the right thing to do.

At first, my mind wasn't on anything but pleasing her the whole night, but before we could go to far, I had a flashback of that night she cried in my arms. That wasn't just a *I had a bad day* cry. That was some heartache she was feeling, and the way she hit that bag let me know she was letting loose some heavy emotions. I didn't feel right trying to move too fast with her physically.

Tremaine and Los went with me to the furniture store to pick up the items I had pre-ordered, then they helped me set up my apartment.

Although we laughed and joked, I was distracted because my mind was still on Kyanah. Would she answer my call later today?

"Yo," Tremaine said, snapping his fingers in my face. "You good man? Los just asked if you wanted to order a pizza."

I snapped out of it. "Oh yeah, sure."

Both of them stared at me for a second but didn't press the situation.

Soon, we were devouring the pizza and watching the game in front of my brand new 105" flatscreen while growing comfortable on my leather couch.

After the game was over, my boys went home and I was left to my own devices.

A lonely feeling swept through me, but it dissipated as I pressed Kyanah's name in my contacts.

She answered on the third ring. "Hello?"

"Hey."

A moment of silence passed before she said, "How are you? Did you get settled into your new apartment?"

Her soft voice tickled my ears. All my prior nervousness about her still being upset with me dissipated, and I cheesed as I answered. "Yeah, Tremaine and Los helped me."

"Did you have to make them some chicken?" she joked, and we shared a brief laugh.

"Nah, I don't think they would like my chicken. I'm not a chef like you."

Her voice lowered an octave. "Boy, hush."

Another brief silence passed before I said, "So Kyanah, I feel like we did this whole thing backward. Tell me more about yourself."

"Huh?" She sounded surprised. "What do you mean, tell you more about myself?"

I shrugged. "I want to know more about you."

"What do you want to know?" She sounded suspicious and I wasn't sure why, but I pressed on.

I kept it casual. "Anything. What do you like to do? Where do you work? Do you have any siblings? That sort of thing."

Kyanah's reluctant tone filled the line. "As you probably know, I like cooking. And music. I already told you at church that I work in human resources. And I have a sister."

She spoke in such a clipped tone, it threw me off. Was she upset with me? I didn't understand why her attitude seemed to resurface.

"Did I catch you at a bad time?" I asked.

A few moments passed before she said, "No. Why?"

I hesitated, then went for it. "You don't seem like you're interested in talking to me."

"Well, we're on the phone, aren't we?"

This conversation wasn't going down the way I hoped. "Listen, I'm tired from the move. I just wanted to check in with you for a few moments. How about we pick back up tomorrow?"

"Okay, that's fine," she said without hesitation and hung up.

I stared at my phone.

What was wrong with Kyanah?

Chapter 19: Kyanah

I should never have let my guard down with Kendrix because now I couldn't stop having flashbacks of me and Terrance's relationship.

Things had progressed too fast between us, just like they did with Kendrix. Except at least me and Terrance had a couple dates before we had sex. Kendrix and I hadn't even exchanged numbers.

The only good thing about last night was that I hadn't slept with Kendrix, but that wasn't even my doing. If Kendrix hadn't stopped, we would have had sex and I would have ended up feeling like an even bigger fool than I already did.

Kendrix looked good and felt good, but he wasn't good for me. I was too vulnerable, just like he said. Now that I had that thought, more doubts clouded my mind and I continued to draw parallels between Terrance and Kendrix, though the men couldn't have been more different.

It was like my heart was putting a wall up to protect me. Kendrix talked a good game and had been consistent so far with how he acted toward me, but what if he switched up like Terrance?

Except I always knew something wasn't right about Terrance. I often got uneasy feelings about him that I swept under the rug, even when my sister Kaliss pointed things out to me. What if I was unintentionally doing the same with Kendrix? My discernment wasn't sharp like it should have been. I needed to pump the brakes on this situationship.

What was wrong with me?

Was I so desperate for a man that I was willing to open my legs to the first one who smiled in my direction?

But the fact that he stopped it before you had sex says something about his character, my mind reasoned. *Plus, he did call you today like he said he would.*

Part of me wanted to hold out hope for me and Kendrix. See where our relationship could go if we took it slow like he suggested.

But another side was ready to call it quits on relationships altogether. If I kept running into the same types of issues, maybe I was the problem.

If Kendrix and I had slept together, this would have been the second time I allowed a man to seduce me before I really wanted to give in to him.

Yes, I lusted over Kendrix, but that didn't mean I genuinely wanted to go through with having sex with him. I needed to get a grip on reality and learn some self-control.

A text buzzed through my phone from Kaliss. *Hey sis. Haven't heard from you in a while. What's up?*

Although I hadn't fully forgiven my sister for not telling me about the kiss she witnessed between Terrance and Stephanie, she wasn't exactly on my shitlist. I was taking things slow with opening back up to her, ironically.

Sighing, I texted back. *Nothing much. Just trying to get through this bullshit anger management and enjoying my kickboxing class.*

Kickboxing? When did you start that?

About a month ago.

Shit, maybe I need to join. I been wanting to put my foot in somebody's ass lately.

That caused me to laugh. *What's wrong with you?*

A few moments passed before she responded. *Ugh, life. These men. Why can't they ever do right?*

Kendrix flashed through my mind once again, but I ignored the thought.

They do have a tendency to fuck up a good thing.

Kaliss called me, which I knew she would do because our text conversations always eventually transitioned to phone calls.

"Hey," she said when I answered. "How have you been feeling lately when it comes to that situation?"

By *that situation,* she was referring to my breakup with Terrance.

"Taking it one day at a time."

"Good, that's all you can do. Meet anybody new lately?"

I tensed. Where had that question come from? I wasn't sure how to answer it. "Not really," I lied, and Kaliss didn't pick up on it.

"Me either. Sooner or later, we're going to meet the right men, sis."

I snorted. "You probably will, before me."

"I doubt it. Have you seen my luck?"

"It's not worse than mine. I waited twenty five years to lose my virginity, only to end up with a nigga who was in love with another woman."

"Kyanah..." she started, trying to comfort me, but I cut her off.

"No, Kaliss. That nigga fucked me over when he did that. I never meant anything to him."

A long silence fell between us after I said that, then Kaliss spoke up again. "You know what sis? Terrance wasn't the right one, and it's undeniable he did you dirty, but you can't lose hope. I strongly believe your day is coming. I hope you believe that too."

I wanted to agree with her, but the more I thought about it, the less hope I had for love in the future.

Chapter 20: Kendrix

At first I was upset at Kyanah for being short with me when we spoke on the phone, but the more I thought about it, the more I realized it was probably for the best.

I pushed up on her, but I meant what I said about not taking advantage.

We moved too fast, point blank. I barely knew anything about her before I was trying to dig in her walls.

The last thing I wanted was to treat her like a rebound.

When Kyanah didn't show up for the next kickboxing session after my move, my heart deflated, but at the same time, it was probably for the best.

I had turned her off by my actions so now I had to take it on the chin.

That was what I got for seducing her, then reneging when she was hot and ready. She probably thought all I was trying to do was play with her mind.

That couldn't be further from the truth, but that was how it looked with the way it went down.

That weekend, Tremaine and Los invited me to their apartment to watch the game. At first I wasn't gonna go because I wanted to stay home in my feelings, then I realized that was a silly thing to do.

When I pulled into the parking lot, my heart leapt at the sight of Kyanah's car parked at the far end.

I stared at it for a few moments before walking up to the building so they could buzz me in.

As I approached the security door to press the button for their apartment, Kyanah walked up the stairs like she was about to leave the building.

She startled when she saw me, then opened the security door. "What are you doing here?" she asked.

I assessed her with my eyes. She was still as beautiful as I remembered and she didn't seem repulsed by my presence, so I smiled.

I nodded toward the stairwell. "I came to watch the game with Tremaine and Los."

She smiled back. "Oh really, that's great!"

"What are you doing?" I couldn't help but ask. "Are you about to go somewhere?"

She shook her head. "No, I was waiting on my sister. She was..."

Just then, the outer door opened and a striking female who looked like Kyanah walked in. "Hey sis," she said, then she looked at me. "Hello...?" Her eyes danced between us.

Kyanah's face reddened. "Kaliss, this is my... friend. Kendrix."

Kaliss gave her a strange look. "Your friend?"

I spoke next. "I used to live in the building. I was just coming back to visit my boys who live upstairs. We're watching the game tonight."

Kaliss nodded.

After I said that, an idea dawned on me. "You know what? Why don't you ladies join us? I'm sure my boys wouldn't mind."

Kyanah looked taken aback by the suggestion, while Kaliss smiled. "Sure, that sounds like a great idea. What do you think, sis?"

The sisters engaged in a brief staring contest before Kyanah conceded.

"Okay, sure," she said. "Let me throw something else on."

"You look fine," Kaliss and I said in unison, and Kaliss gave me a smile. I liked Kyanah's sister.

Kyanah blushed, then instead of taking the stairs like usual, I joined the sisters on the elevator.

We engaged in small talk as we rose to the fourth floor, then when we approached Tremaine and Los' door, I couldn't help but smirk before knocking.

They had been ragging on me about losing my touch with women and said I was gonna be using a walker before I found another one.

When Los opened the door, his expression was priceless. "Kyanah!" he said, his jaw dropping as he looked from me, to Kyanah, then her sister. "And who is this beautiful woman with you?"

At the mention of a beautiful woman, Tremaine appeared at the door. He had recently ended things with his little jumpoff, but from the way he was eyeing Kaliss, he wasn't upset about it. "My my my," he said. "Don't be rude, Los. Invite our guests inside."

We entered their apartment and Tremaine and Los were on their best behavior. "Would you ladies like a drink?" Tremaine asked.

Kyanah blushed and her sister giggled. "Sure," Kaliss said, and from the way she eyed Tremaine when his back was turned to pour the drinks, there was chemistry igniting between them.

"I'm about to order a pizza," Los said next, not to be outdone with hospitality. "Kyanah, why don't you choose the toppings since we still owe you a welcome meal?"

Tremaine chuckled as he handed the ladies their drinks, allowing his hand to linger on Kaliss' when he handed her hers.

"Welcome meal?" Kaliss said, when she finished staring at Tremaine. She turned to Kyanah. "What's that about?"

Kyanah rolled her eyes and explained while Los called the pizza spot to place the order.

Kyanah told him what toppings she wanted and they said they would be there soon.

It was comical seeing my boys go all out for Kyanah and her sister, and it was probably clear to everyone in the room that Tremaine and Kaliss were feeling each other.

As for me and Kyanah, we didn't say much to each other, but she did snuggle up against me on the couch and when the game was over, she told me to call her when I got home.

Los watched the girls as they walked toward the elevator then closed the door, immediately staring at me. "Nigga!" he said, his eyes wide with glee. "Let me find out."

Tremaine gave me a playful jab. "And why you ain't tell me she had a sister? Had me out here looking like a scrub trying to impress her."

I chuckled. "That's what y'all get for talking all that shit."

Chapter 21: Kyanah

Things were looking up for me and Kendrix.

While we were watching the game together, I realized I was being silly by not giving the man a chance. He told me repeatedly he wanted to take it slow and instead of hearing him, my mind immediately jumped to doubt and fear.

I wasn't going to allow those emotions to rule me anymore. What happened to Terrance was in the past. I couldn't let his actions ruin my potential future with Kendrix.

Kaliss seemed to like Kendrix too. "Sis, why didn't you tell me you met someone?" she said, looking giddy with excitement when we entered the elevator from leaving Tremaine and Los' apartment.

I tried to play it off at first. "It looked like you and Tremaine hit it off nicely."

She blushed, but refocused like she knew what I was trying to do. "This is not about me. What's up with you and Kendrix?"

The way she said his name let me know how she felt about him.

I shrugged. "Some things have happened between us, but we're taking it slow."

"What things?" Her eyes flashed with excitement. "I like him for you. Tell me everything."

The elevator doors dinged as my eyes widened with surprise. "What do you mean, you like him for me?" But I couldn't help but smile at the revelation.

She shrugged as we walked off and entered the main lobby for her to leave. "I just get a good feeling from him, is all."

I studied my sister. Kaliss had never said that about Terrance. In fact, the only thing she ever did when it came to him was warn me to be careful.

What was so different about Kendrix? My mind filled with questions, but I was too tired to discuss it right then.

"Call me when you get home," I said, then she smiled again.

We shared a hug before she left. "Don't stay up too late talking to Kendrix now." She winked as she exited the building.

I watched her as she walked to her car, then stood there until she pulled out of her space, honking and waving before driving off.

After that, I returned to my apartment, going over the night in my head. I took my shower and slipped into my silk pajamas, entering my bedroom and remembering how Kendrix's lips and hands felt all over me.

In the middle of my lustful reminiscing, Kaliss texted me. *Did he call yet? I'm home.*

I didn't know why she was so pressed for me and Kendrix to talk, but I couldn't deny that I liked the fact that my sister felt Kendrix was good for me.

I hoped she was right.

Not yet, I said, then right after I pressed Send, a call came through from him. Giddiness filled my heart and I pressed the green button.

"Hello?" I answered.

Movement sounded in the background, like Kendrix was driving. His smooth, baritone voice filled my eardrum. "I couldn't wait til I got home before I called," he said. "How have you been, girl?"

I cheesed. "I been good. Hope you're driving safe."

"I am," he said as I texted Kaliss to let her know I was on the phone with him.

Yayyyy! she responded before I returned to my conversation.

"You all settled in?" Kendrix asked, and I laid back with my head on my pillow, staring at the ceiling as I responded.

"Sure am. Just got out of the shower."

I heard his blinker clicking as he spoke his next words. "Is that right? Well I won't keep you up too late."

"I don't mind talking for a little while."

A silence fell between us. I was unsure of where to take the conversation and I had a hunch he felt the same.

"Listen, I'm sorry for being short with you," I was saying, while he said, "Kyanah, I need to tell you something."

"Go ahead," he said.

"I just wanted to apologize for being short with you the last time we talked," I said. "You have been nothing but nice to me since we met, but after what happened, I got scared."

"Me too," he said. "I didn't want you to think I was playing with your mind, but I felt like I owed you more than just trying to jump your bones before I moved out of the building."

I giggled at the imagery. "I honestly wouldn't have minded, but I am glad we stopped. Now we can get to know each other for real."

"Right." I heard movement on his end like he was exiting his car.

"You home?" I asked.

"Yup, walking up to the door now."

A few more moments of silence passed as he entered his apartment, then he spoke up again. "So let's try this again. Tell me about yourself, Kyanah."

I grinned. "Actually, it's your turn, Kendrix. Last time, I answered all the questions but you didn't tell me anything about yourself. What made you teach the kickboxing class?"

"I guess it is my turn," he said with a chuckle. "But I started teaching the class because it was always something I was into. Their used to be a men's class too, but that one fizzled out and the women seemed to be the ones who gravitated more toward it."

"Hm, I wonder why?" I mused as I thought about my reasons for attending.

"I can imagine," he replied. "But I enjoy the class. I like teaching and seeing women empowered. Plus it doesn't hurt to know that what I'm teaching can serve as a form of protection against niggas who try funny shit."

"That's true," I said, not considering that aspect of the class. "You're a good teacher," I added.

I could hear the smile in his voice as he answered. "Thank you. You're a good student."

"Did you grow up in the church?" I suddenly remembered the day I met his mother.

Kendrix explained to me how he went to church with his mom and dad growing up until his dad passed, and it made me grow a deeper appreciation for him. He was sexy and Godfearing. A dangerous combination. I shared more about myself after that, and we talked for another hour before we both were ready for bed, then we proceeded to call and text each other every day for the next few weeks.

We hadn't gone out on a date yet, but I knew it was only a matter of time before he would ask.

In the meantime, I returned to the kickboxing classes and continued my journey there.

After checking myself out in the mirror some time later, I realized the class was paying off in more ways than one. My arms were becoming toned, and my back and waist were snatched.

"Go me!" I said, twerking at my reflection, then I burst out laughing. It felt good to laugh again.

***

Kaliss and I went out to lunch to catch up on life and hang out.

"Girl, so tell me what happened between you and Tremaine," I gushed, as we sat in our seats.

Kaliss blushed and I knew she had good news. "He is so sexy, Kyanah. Like damn!"

My mind flashed to Tremaine. He was sexy with that blemish-free brown skin and those tattoos going up his arm, not to mention his charming personality. I liked Tremaine for my sister. Hopefully he was the one for her.

"Where did he take you?" I asked, and Kaliss' smile widened again. She opened her mouth to tell me, but something behind me caught her attention. Her face fell and her eyes narrowed, then she crossed her arms and gave a stank look to whoever was behind us.

I turned around and got the shock of my life when I saw Stephanie and Terrance standing there. Stephanie's bump was showing and a feeling of pain swept through me before it dissipated. I stared at her smug expression, then focused on my sister. "Let's go somewhere else," I said. I hadn't thought about them in what felt like ages and they were not about to fuck up our good day. I shouldn't have had to leave the restaurant, but they still had a restraining order on me. Though Kaliss and I were here first, I could tell from the look in Stephanie's eyes she was ready to make this situation into a headache.

Kaliss seemed to agree with my decision to leave. She grabbed her purse and we stood and walked toward Stephanie and Terrance, who were standing near the hostesses' station. Terrance was eyeing me like a piece of meat and it made me feel disgusted. I know he didn't think I would ever go back to his tired ass, especially not with his pregnant girlfriend standing right next to him.

"Yeah, that's right, go somewhere else," Stephanie taunted as we approached. "We don't need your ratchet ass tearing up the restaurant because you can't control your temper."

"Bitch, who the hell are you calling ratchet?" Kaliss said, stepping forward.

I held my sister back. "Don't bother sis, she's not worth it. Any woman who needs to throw her relationship in another woman's face is obviously insecure."

"I'm not throwing..." Stephanie started, but Kaliss and I exited the restaurant while she was still talking.

Chapter 22: Kendrix

My mother had been pestering me the past couple weeks about inviting Kyanah to Sunday dinner. I tried to explain to her that we were just getting to know each other and hadn't even had our first date yet, but Ma wasn't hearing none of that. Her suspicious tone filled my eardrums as we spoke on the phone. "What, are you ashamed of me or something?" she said. "I haven't seen her back at church since that one time she came."

"Ma, she was just visiting. She probably has a different church home." I didn't know that for sure, since me and Kyanah hadn't discussed her church background, but I thought it would get my mother off my back. It didn't.

"I'm serious, Kendrix. I want to see your friend. I get a good feeling about her."

That threw me for a loop. "How so?"

She was silent for a second. "Don't worry about all of that. It's a woman's intuition. Go on and text her and invite her. Now."

I sighed and obliged my mother's request, shooting Kyanah a text and hoping I wasn't about to embarrass myself by her turning me down.

Hey... my mother has a request.

She texted back a few moments later. *Your mother? What kind of request?*

"Did you text her?" Ma's voice filled the line.

"Yes, Ma!" I pretended to be annoyed but I was secretly excited that Kyanah hadn't immediately shot me down.

She wants you to come to Sunday dinner. I pressed Send.

"What did she say?" Ma's voice chimed in again.

"Can you give her a chance to answer?" I replied, as Kyanah's response came through.

Sure. What is she cooking?

"She asked what you're cooking," I said before Ma could ask me again if she responded.

"Tell her I said fried chicken, yams, macaroni and cheese, and green beans."

I relayed the message through text.

Kyanah wrote back immediately. *I'll be there with bells on!*

"She said yes," I responded, and my mother let off a squeal of delight while the nervous tension I felt when waiting for Kyanah's response dissipated.

Chapter 23: Kyanah

I agreed to Sunday dinner at Kendrix's mother's house partially to be polite and the other reason was because I liked the woman. She was friendly to me when I visited their church and from the way Kendrix spoke about her, I could tell he was close with his mother.

But as Sunday loomed closer, I grew nervous. What was I supposed to wear? How should I style my hair? Should I wear makeup? I had worn light makeup when I visited Kendrix's church and his mother seemed pleased by my appearance when she gave me a onceover, so I went with a similar dress for Sunday dinner.

Kendrix offered to pick me up, but I was nervous about how the evening would go so I made up a lie about having something to do before the dinner and said I would meet him there.

When I pulled up to his mother's street, I was happy to see his car was already parked outside. That meant I wouldn't be subjected to possible awkward conversation while we waited for him to arrive.

I grabbed my pot with potholders and carefully carried it toward the front door.

I was just wondering how I was going to hold onto the hot and heavy pan and knock at the same time when the front door opened and Kendrix and his mother appeared on the porch.

Her eyes lit up at the sight of my pot. "What do you have there?"

I beamed, happy that I had made the right decision to bring a dish. That was another thing I had agonized over. At first, I was going to bring a dessert, but then I imagined she probably was already planning a dessert, so I opted for collard greens. "I wanted to thank you for your kind gesture," I replied as Kendrix rushed down the steps to take the pot from me. "I know you already made green beans, but I figured collard greens wouldn't hurt to add."

Her jaw dropped. "Collard greens? Don't tell me you can cook now!"

I gave her a bashful shrug as I walked up the steps. "I do a little something."

We shared a brief hug.

"Don't let her lie to you, Ma," Kendrix said, seemingly pleased by the way his mother and I were interacting. "Wait til you taste her fried chicken."

After he said that, Kendrix and I shared a knowing look. I remembered that first night we met and he acted like he didn't want my chicken. He fixed me with a smirk and licked his lips, then led the way to the kitchen. When he set the pot on the stove, his mother walked over to open it while Kendrix pulled me in his arms for an embrace. He smelled so good it made my mouth water.

What shocked me more was the light kiss he laid on my lips while his mother's back was turned, then he stepped back with another smirk, still holding one of my hands before he let it drop.

"These greens smell good, honey!" Beverly said and turned to me with a smile.

"I hope you like them."

"I'm sure we will. Go on, you and Kendrix sit down and I'll fix the plates."

Kendrix and I agreed, sitting across from each other. He stared into my eyes like he was studying for a test, and his gaze was so intense it made me heat up inside. If he didn't stop looking at me like that I was going to jump across this table and straddle him.

Beverly placed a plate before me, then one before Kendrix, before returning to the counter to grab her plate.

After she sat down, she glanced between me and her son with a smile before she gestured at Kendrix.

"Say grace."

We bowed our heads and held hands as Kendrix blessed the food, then we dug in.

My stomach was somersaulting at the possibility of Beverly not liking my collard greens, but she laid her fork down and gave me a look of approval. "Girl, what did you put in these greens?"

I giggled. "You like them?"

"I sure do! They remind me of my grandmother's."

That warmed my heart because it let me know her response was genuine.

The more the meal wore on, the more comfortable I felt. Being with Kendrix and his mother felt natural, like I belonged.

Chapter 24: Kendrix

I was ready to take things to the next level with Kyanah. Now that her and Ma had hit it off so nicely, I was itching to take her out on a date.

All our conversations had been good, and she was excelling in the kickboxing class too. Kyanah had even signed up for a mock tournament. It was more of a display of moves than an actual match, but there were cash prizes for nailing the techniques.

I was elated when she told me she was signing up.

Bianca and Alena signed up too. It made me proud to see that the group of ladies I had been training had that much confidence in what I taught them that they wanted to share it with the world.

I shouldn't have been nervous to just call and ask Kyanah on a date or send a message through text, but I wanted to ask in person.

I got the funny feeling we were making a big step toward something beautiful. My heart screamed that this wasn't some average relationship, and that what Kyanah and I had was real.

I only hoped she felt the same.

We had another successful class, where I showed them a new combination and everyone got it by the end of the night. After class, I hung back as Kyanah took her shower.

When she emerged from the locker room, she seemed surprised to see me. "What are you still doing here?"

I grinned. "Waiting on you."

She eyed me. "For what?"

"I wanted to ask you something."

Her eyes widened. "Ask me what?"

My grin widened. "I wanted to ask if you could make me some more chicken."

A look of confusion crossed her features before she rolled her eyes and punched my arm. "Boy, stop. You and your jokes about that chicken. It must have been legendary."

"I admit it was."

She cocked her head at me. "Why'd you turn it down when I asked if you wanted more then?"

I shrugged. "I needed to teach you a lesson."

She smirked. "A lesson, huh?"

We exited the building walking side by side. I held the door for her, then allowed it to close after us. "Yup," I responded. "You were a bad girl and I had to set you straight."

She pursed her lips and I wanted to kiss them. "Whatever. Anyway, what did you really want to talk to me about?"

We headed to our cars in the parking lot. "I wanna take you out."

She pretended not to understand. "Take me out? Damn, Kendrix, I thought we were on good terms."

It was my turn to give her a playful nudge. "Come on girl, you know what I mean. Will you go out on a date with me?"

I licked my lips as I awaited her response.

She stared at me with a neutral expression before her face broke out into a beautiful smile. "I thought you'd never ask."

Chapter 25: Kyanah

Kendrix and I saw each other every week and talked and texted all day long on the phone, so I didn't know why I was so nervous to see him. Especially after we had such a good time at Sunday dinner with his mother too. I didn't know why my mind was still doubting our connection. We were taking things slow, but it still felt like it was going too smooth. Like I was waiting for the other shoe to drop and for Kendrix to take off his mask and turn into Terrance. It was irrational, I knew it, because Kendrix had shown me time and time again that he was nothing like Terrance, but I couldn't help my fear. At the same time, I couldn't squelch my excitement about what was happening between us.

I stared at myself in the mirror, wearing a form-fitting red dress and heels. I took some time to apply a full face of makeup and had gotten my hair and nails done earlier that day. A giddy feeling swept through me as I thought about how I had pulled out all stops to get ready for this date.

Spraying my Chanel perfume, I gave myself one more assessment in the mirror, my eyes sweeping up and down my body before I surmised that I was one bad bitch. It wasn't because of Kendrix. It was because of me.

I had worked hard over the past couple months to get over Stephanie and Terrance and I was proud to say that I barely thought about them anymore. That was huge for me because at one point, all I thought about was what I went through with them.

The anger management classes had ended a week ago and I couldn't have been happier. Once I finished, I realized that the sessions weren't that bad. I just wasn't in the right headspace when the group was forced upon me. They taught some great tools to people who needed them.

The night after the class ended, I got a random message on social media from Stephanie, gloating about how she was six months along and asking how my classes were going.

I didn't know why that bitch was so obsessed with me, but I blocked her and Terrance from my phone and all social media, which was something I should have done a long time ago.

After I blocked them, I remembered the restraining order and half-wished I had screenshotted the conversation so I could send it to the judge, but the more I thought about it, the more I realized she wasn't worth it.

Why go back there when my life had taken such a positive turn?

The buzzer rang, which let me know Kendrix was outside. My heart swelled with excitement once more and I smoothed out my dress, shimmied my shoulders, and flipped off the light.

Taking the short flight up the stairs, I caught the sight of Kendrix standing behind the security door. He was dressed nicely in fresh pressed slacks, a crisp dress shirt, and Stacey Adams shoes. When I opened the door to greet him with a hug, I caught a whiff of his cologne. The man smelled damn good.

His white teeth flashed in a smile and that was the moment when I realized he had his arm behind his back.

"What are you hiding?" I giggled.

His smirk widened, then he showed me.

A dozen red roses were displayed before me.

When I saw them, I gasped, then looked up into his eyes. "Those are for me?"

He nodded and gestured for me to take them.

I did, and when I inhaled their scent it brought a tear to my eyes.

"You like?" he asked, studying my expression.

I blinked back the tears. Kendrix had no idea what he had just done. I had been on a number of dates with men and a three-year relationship with Terrance, and not one of them had ever bought me flowers. "Thank you."

Kendrix held the outer door open for me, then we walked down the stairs. His car was parked right outside the building. I blushed as he opened the passenger side door for me to get in. I nervously clicked my seatbelt and settled in as he hopped in the driver's side. The smooth leather seats felt like butter and the temperature and music were set at the perfect volume.

As we rode down the city streets toward our destination, I couldn't stop looking at the roses and staring up at the starry sky.

Sometimes it was the little things.

Chapter 26: Kendrix

All the nervousness I felt about me and Kyanah going on our first official date erased as soon as I saw her smile.

We pulled up to the restaurant and I told her to wait, then opened the door for her when she got out of the car. She blushed at me when I did that like she wasn't used to that type of treatment. I couldn't wait to show her more. When we entered the restaurant, I held the door for her again, then she was shocked to find that I had already made reservations for us.

What kind of niggas was she dealing with before me? I wondered, but they didn't matter now. It was time to show her how a man was supposed to treat a woman. My father had taught me well by the way he treated my mother and I had always treated my women right, including Jazzmyne, but none of them made me feel the way Kyanah did.

The waitress approached our table to ask what we wanted for drinks. I looked at Kyanah for her to choose. She stared at the menu for a second, then said, "I'll have a glass of Merlot."

I agreed. "We'll take a bottle."

When that was settled, the waitress walked away and I stared at the beautiful woman sitting across from me.

Her cheeks reddened. "Why are you always looking at me like that?"

"Like what?" I said, not breaking eye contact.

"Like you wanna eat me or something."

I chuckled. "Would you make it nervous if I said that was exactly what I wanted to do?"

That only made her blush more, so I chuckled again and let up.

The waitress returned and poured our drinks from the bottle.

When she walked away, Kyanah glanced around at the soft imagery and chandeliered ceilings. "This is a nice place."

"Only the best for you."

As the night wore on, Kyanah and I had a great conversation. She shared with me about how her sister and Tremaine seemed to be getting close, then she looked at me for hints that he felt the same. "He seems to really like her," I offered, and Kyanah relaxed. "Why? What's up?"

She shook her head. "Nothing, it's just... I really hope it works out for them."

There was weight behind her words but I wasn't here to ponder Tremaine and Kaliss' future.

"Where do you see yourself in five years?" I asked out of the blue.

Her face scrunched for a second before it registered. Then she pondered for a moment. "Definitely married, probably with a kid or two. You?" Now it was her turn to give me an intense stare like I had been giving her.

Her eyes were doing something to me, but I kept it cool. "Pretty much the same. I'm ready to settle down."

When I said that, a silence fell between us. My mind went to everything that happened with Jazzmyne and how I thought me and her would end up married and having children of our own, but it didn't work out that way. From the expression on Kyanah's face, she likely was thinking on similar lines.

After our meal was over, we weren't ready for the night to end, so we went to the city's boardwalk to park and chat some more. On the way back to my car, Kyanah complained that her feet were hurting, so I scooped her up on my back and carried her the rest of the way.

"You better not drop me!" Kyanah giggled in my ear, and I pretended I was about to for a second before quickly recovering.

"Kendrix!" she squealed, clapping me on my back.

That was a good night, and our second date was even better. Kyanah had mentioned that she'd never been on a cruise, so I found a three-hour lunch cruise in a neighboring city and booked it for us.

Her eyes lit up with excitement as she saw the boat.

"Kendrix!" she said, and I decided I liked the way my name sounded on her lips.

While on the ship, she gazed out at the water while we chatted and ate, then we walked the ship's perimeter hand in hand.

During the final hour, there was a dance party and Kyanah and I danced and slow grinded to most of the songs. She was turning me on with the sexy way she was looking at me, but my heart told me there was something deeper at work.

I was falling in love.

I had been in love before with Jazzmyne, but there was something different about what I felt for Kyanah. What we had was pure.

Tonight, Kyanah said she was surprising me with a date.

This was a first because I usually was the one to take a woman out, not the other way around. I had never had a woman treat me, and it felt weird, but in a good way.

Kyanah picked me up at my place and she was looking beautiful as ever in her ass-hugging jeans and jersey.

"Remember this?" she asked, gesturing at the jersey.

I wasn't following, but I nodded like I did anyway.

Kyanah giggled and slapped my arm. "It's the female version of the jersey you were wearing the first night we met, silly!"

My eyes lit up as realization dawned, then I studied how her breasts poked out through the form-fitting top.

I licked my lips. "I must admit, yours fits you better."

She smiled and we headed to the arcade. When we walked inside, I turned to her with a cocky grin. "What do you want to get beat at first?"

Kyanah cocked her head to the side. "Boy bye. What, you thought this jersey was for nothing? I'm about to wipe the floor with your ass."

My eyes widened in amusement at the challenge. "Word? You talking big shit, girl. Let's see if you can back it up."

Kyanah surprised me by beating me at our very first game, which was table hockey. I should have known it was about to be on from the way she put her game face on when it started, but I quickly found out she was not to be fucked with. She beat me three times in a row in that game, though I lied and said I let her win, just to get under her skin.

"Whatever baby," she said. "That ain't nothing but ego."

I chuckled, then my eyes caught a woman across the room staring daggers in Kyanah's direction. Who was this chick?

Kyanah noticed my change in expression. "What is it?" she asked, then followed my gaze.

She stiffened at the sight of the woman, then turned back to me. "I hope she doesn't start shit with me while we're having so much fun."

"Who is that?"

She sighed. "Her name is Stephanie. The reason I moved into Tremaine and Los' building was because I caught her fucking my ex in our bed." Kyanah briefly ran down the story about the woman who seemed to be obsessed with trying to rub betrayal in Kyanah's face. As she told the story, a dude walked up to Stephanie and put his arm around her, and before Kyanah could open her mouth, I answered for her.

"That must be Terrance, huh?"

She nodded.

I saw she was getting worked up, so I cupped her chin and turned her face to mine, staring in her eyes. "Don't even worry about them, baby. Fuck them. It's about me and you now."

She stared at me til she calmed down and I pressed my lips against hers.

Our kiss deepened and she wrapped her arms around my neck while I wrapped my arms around her waist, pulling her closer.

By the time we finished kissing, she had forgotten all about that chick.

We played some more games at the arcade. I busted Kyanah's ass at the hoop game, then we played a racing game next.

She was in first place, while I was in second, but I wasn't about to take that L. At the last moment, I wrenched her wheel to the side while holding mine steady and won the race.

"Ew, you cheater!" she said, slapping my arm.

I gave her a mischievous grin, then leaned in and kissed her lips. "Come on baby, I couldn't let you do me like that."

She rolled her eyes. "Whatever. Sore losing ass."

We played a few more games until the arcade was about to close. I kept my head on a swivel to look out for Stephanie and Terrance in case they came over to start trouble with us, but thankfully, I didn't see them again after that first time.

When we got back to my place, I wanted to know more about what happened to her. "Not to get you upset or anything, but what happened with your ex?"

Kyanah seemed taken aback by my question. She sighed, then went through the whole story, tearing up at times, while my fists curled in anger.

When she finished, I realized we had a lot more in common than I thought.

"Damn baby," I said. "Our pasts are so similar." I told her what happened with me and Jazzmyne and by the time I finished my story, Kyanah's jaw was on the floor.

"Kendrix, I'm so sorry!" she said, reaching out to give me a hug. "Are you okay?"

I nodded. "I'm good now. The only thing that still hurts a little is that I never got to say goodbye to Kanai, but maybe we'll catch up when he gets older, if he still remembers me."

"I'm sure he will," she encouraged, then a curious look crossed her features. "How many kids do you want?"

I thought about it. "Probably two. A boy and a girl, maybe. You?"

She smiled. "The same. Maybe if things go right between us, we'll have our own children."

I smiled back, my heart fluttering at the possibility. Me and Kyanah would make some beautiful ass babies. "Maybe."

We shared another kiss.

Chapter 27: Kyanah

Three months later...

I stared at the gift box, then at Kendrix's smiling face. "Go ahead, open it," he urged.

It was my birthday and Kendrix had treated me all day long. We went to the spa and got a couple's massage, then we went out for brunch, then caught a movie, then we went back to the boardwalk, then dinner, and now, he said he had a gift for me.

From the looks and rectangular shape of the tiny box, it was jewelry. But he had already done so much for me.

I didn't want to compare, but I couldn't help but to notice the stark differences between the way Terrance had treated me during our three-year relationship, and the way Kendrix had swept me off my feet in a matter of months.

This man surprised me more every day and I was grateful for it.

It was like we were meant to be, like we fit.

I slowly pulled the top of the box off and stared at the sparkling jewels on the bracelet. "Wow, Kendrix, it's beautiful!" I gushed.

He pulled it out, then I extended my wrist so he could clasp it. It fit perfectly.

"Thank you!" I wrapped my arms around his neck and kissed him.

"Now when my birthday comes around, I want a Ferrari," he joked.

I pushed his head. "Boy please."

When the amusement died down, I fixed him with a solemn expression. "I really appreciate you going all out for me. No man has ever made me feel the way you do."

He nodded. "Same here. You're someone special, Kyanah."

We leaned into each other for a kiss, then pulled back.

I had ideas for how this night could end off right, but I wasn't sure if Kendrix would be down. The chemistry between us had been steadily building, but he hadn't tried to make a move on me sexually yet. He made little jokes about things he wanted to do in the bedroom, but he hadn't grabbed me up like he did that night at my apartment. Steamy thoughts filled my mind, but I didn't want to broach the topic in case he wasn't ready. Last time we got hot and heavy, he stopped it. I would die if that happened again.

We were sitting in his car in the restaurant parking lot, staring up at the sky and continuing our conversation.

"How's your mom doing?" I asked.

Kendrix had been staring straight ahead, but he turned to me when I asked that. "She's good. She asked about you."

"Really? What did she say?"

"She wants to know when you're coming back to church."

I searched his eyes. "What did you tell her?"

He shrugged. "That you're a heathen and would prefer Satan's temple."

I sucked my teeth and swatted his arm. "Asshole."

He chuckled. "I'm just playing. I told her you will visit again soon."

I leaned in and snuggled up against him. "That I will."

Kendrix and I spent another hour together before he brought me home.

After settling in, I called Kaliss to check on her because I hadn't heard from her in a couple of days. We had hung out last weekend for my birthday since Kendrix was taking me out today, but I hadn't received a call or text from her yet.

"Hello?" she answered, sounding stressed.

"What's wrong with you?" I asked.

"These clients. They can be quite demanding at times."

My sister was a real estate attorney and often had wild stories of the stuff she had to deal with when it came to her clients. Many of them wanted perfection while barely coming to the table with their ducks in order.

"Maybe you should go on vacation," I suggested.

Kaliss spoke in a faraway tone. "I wish."

"Seriously, sis. You work hard. You need to take time off. Your clients will be there when you come back."

Kaliss was silent for a moment. "Wanna come with me?"

My heart leapt at her suggestion. "Actually, yeah. I'm down! Ever since Kendrix took me on that day cruise I've been wanting to do an overnight one. How about we book it together? We can also bring Mom."

"Bring Mom?" Kaliss sounded mortified at the thought. "Girl, I'm trying to get drunk and have fun half naked on a boat. Why on Earth would I invite our mother?"

I giggled. "Damn, Kaliss, I'm telling Mommy you dissed her."

"Whatever."

"Anyway, let's look into it because I wanna go to Mexico."

"Hmm..." Kalis said, sounding like she was typing as she spoke. "Actually, I was thinking Cuba."

"I'm down either way. Just let me know when."

"They have some nice looking ones coming up soon. How about next month?"

"Cool."

I was about to say something else when Kaliss chimed back in. "Oh, sis, I meant to tell you! But first, happy birthday! I can't believe I forgot to text you."

"You're good; we hung out over the weekend. Tell me what?"

She let out an evil laugh. "You will never guess who broke up."

"Who?" I racked my brains, trying to think of mutual friends who Kaliss would be laughing about their breakup.

"Your ex and his ex baby momma."

My mind swirled. "Come again?"

Kaliss chuckled. "Apparently, the baby Stephanie raved about wasn't Terrance's. Apparently, she was kicking it with some other nigga behind his back. They had it all over social media. Terrance went Live blasting her, and she went Live trying to defend herself, then random people started chiming in, egging on their arguments."

"Wow." I was surprised at that one, especially since Stephanie seemed obsessed with rubbing their relationship and baby in my face.

"You want me to send you screenshots?" Kaliss asked.

I thought about it for a second. "Nah, I'm done with them and their drama. Whatever happened, they had it coming."

"I know that's right."

Chapter 28: Kendrix

Kyanah and I had a great time for her birthday. I enjoyed spoiling her, especially since she told me about how her ex never did shit for her. When I got home, I was exhausted from the day's events, so all I wanted to do was take a shower and go to sleep.

I trudged to my bathroom and let the steam fill the room as the hot water gushed from the faucet. I stood underneath it, lathering my body from head to toe. Visions of the night me and Kyanah almost sealed the deal ran through my mind, and I wanted to invite her over or go back over to her place to end the night off right.

I wondered if she would be down?

We had been together for a minute. We had taken it slow like we both said we wanted, but now my body was telling me it wanted more.

Emerging from the shower, a blast of cool air hit me while I dried off.

After I finished in the bathroom, I returned to my bedroom and saw that my phone was lit up with a call.

By the time I reached my nightstand, the ring had run out, but the hairs on the back of my neck stood up when I saw that there were nine missed calls.

My heart jumped in my chest and my first thought was of Kyanah. Had something happened? I snatched up my phone to see who called me and saw that it was Jazzmyne.

"Jazzmyne?" I scrunched up my face. Why the hell was she blowing up my phone after all this time?

I didn't want to answer, and I was about to block her - something I should have done a long time ago - when a text came through from her.

Please answer, Kendrix. I think he's gonna kill us!

Kill us? Kill who?

Sucking my teeth, I called her back.

"Hello?" she answered on the first ring, her voice sounding jittery and frantic.

"What are you talking about, Jazzmyne?"

"It's Sky!" she wailed. "He's crazy! He's been hitting me and ... we tried to get away. He beat Kanai too. Oh my God, my baby...."

My heart dropped. "What's wrong with Kanai? Is he okay?"

She calmed down to answer. "He's okay but Sky made him bleed. There are bruises all over his back. Kendrix, can we please stay with you tonight?"

"What?" I wasn't comprehending the situation.

One minute, I never thought I would hear from Jazzmyne or Kanai again and the next, she was calling and asking if they could stay with me.

"Please, Kendrix!" she screamed in my ear. "Can you please come get us before he comes back home?"

"Why don't you call the police?"

"Because that shit ain't gonna work! I already got a restraining order on him before but he ignores it. He thinks because he pays the bills he can come in here whenever he wants. Please, Kendrix, I don't have anybody else who can help me." She sounded desperate and that wasn't something I had ever experienced with Jazzmyne.

I didn't trust this shit. My gut was telling me that this situation was all wrong, especially with the way she came to me out of nowhere. But if something happened to Kanai and I could have prevented it, I wouldn't be able to forgive myself.

I sighed, not believing I was about to get involved in this bullshit. "Where are you, Jazzmyne?"

"I'm at home..." She whimpered. "Are you coming?"

I shook my head. "I'm not meeting you at your house. Can you make it to a more neutral location?"

Silence filled the line for a few moments.

"I could probably make it to the drug store up on the corner."

"Okay I'll be there in a second."

When I hung up with her, I threw some clothes on and dialed Tremaine and Los to meet me there. I didn't know what type of niggas Sky ran with or what he could be into, so in case this was some kind of ambush, I wanted my boys with me.

They both said they were down.

The whole time over there, I wanted to bust a U-turn, call Jazzmyne, and tell her I couldn't help her and that she needed to call the police. But Kanai's face kept flashing in my mind. I never even got the chance to say goodbye to him after helping to raise him for three years. If he was in trouble and I didn't do anything to help him, I wouldn't be able to live with that decision.

Tremaine, Los, and I arrived at the drug store near Jazzmyne's apartment around the same time as each other and thankfully, the only people who were outside were random customers going in and out of the store, and Jazzmyne and Kanai.

Both of them looked shaken. Jazzmyne's lip was busted, her shirt was ripped, and half her hair was pulled out. Her scalp was bleeding. Kanai was limping and his clothing looked ruffled too. I immediately wanted to find that nigga Sky and murk him, but this wasn't my battle. Jazzmyne wasn't my woman and Kanai wasn't my son. I was here to help her for a night and that was it.

Jazzmyne was carrying two duffel bags that were stuffed with items.

I looked at Tremaine and Los and both of them wore grim expressions, likely having similar thoughts as me about what Sky had done.

"I understand this is some crazy shit, but that ain't your fight, bruh," Tremaine said, as if hearing my thoughts.

"He's right," Los said under his breath. "Do what you can for her tonight but that's it. Don't get tangled up with this bitch again."

"Gotchu," I responded as I held open the door for Kanai to get in first and made sure he was secure, then held the other door open for Jazzmyne.

"Thank you," she said with a sniffle as we pulled out of the parking lot with Tremaine and Los traveling close behind.

I didn't respond to her. I glanced in the rearview at Kanai, who was eerily silent. It broke my heart. "We gotta get him to a hospital," I said, and was about to flick my blinker when Jazzmyne jerked and put her hand on the wheel. Her eyes widened in fear. "No! We can't go to the hospital!"

I was startled by her sudden gesture. "Why not? He could have internal bleeding or some shit, and you don't look too good either."

"I just want to get away from that house, Kendrix. I will take Kanai to the hospital once I know he's safe. If we go there now, Sky will find us."

I didn't agree with that decision, but it wasn't my choice to make.

I glanced at Kanai again. "You hungry little man?" I fought back a tear at the sight of him.

He just stared at me blankly, then shook his head.

"He's been like that all day," she said. "I don't know what made Sky do that to us but I'm leaving him. Things haven't been right since he got out, Kendrix. Since you left us."

You mean, since you kicked me out? I wanted to say, but I wasn't here for an argument. "Where do you want me to take y'all?" I asked, because although she asked to stay with me when we spoke on the phone, that wasn't happening. "Your mom's crib?"

She shook her head. "No, Sky will find us there."

"One of your cousins?"

She shook her head again.

I tried not to be frustrated. "Where do you want to go, Jazzmyne?"

Her next words came out in a small voice. "Can't we stay with you? Just for the night."

I couldn't believe her nerve. I understood she was hurting and scared, and I would never respect a man who put his hands on a woman, but for her to ask to stay at my crib was wild.

"I don't think that's a good idea. I'll rent y'all a hotel room."

"No!" she exclaimed, and her eyes widened with fear. "I can't go to a hotel. He'll find us. That's what happened last time."

"Last time?" I said, trying to keep the bass out of my voice as I spoke. "How many times has this happened before, Jazzmyne?"

She stared at me, which I caught from the corner of my eye. "The first few times, it was only me that he hit."

Damn. This story was more fucked up by the minute.

"Listen, have you spoken to the police?" I already asked about the police earlier, but the more I heard, the less I wanted to do with this situation.

"No, he would kill us, Kendrix!"

"You still should file a report and tell them he broke the restraining order. Y'all need to go to a hospital too. I understand you're scared, but there could be hidden injuries you need to address."

Jazzmyne shook her head. "I don't trust the police. Plus, he only sees a restraining order as a piece of paper. I planned to go to my sister's house in the morning. We only need to stay with you for tonight."

I didn't like the fact that Jazzmyne felt like she had me at her disposal, despite her situation. She seemed to have forgotten about how dirty she had done me, and she seemed confident that I would let her stay with me, regardless of how many times I protested. It disgusted me that she

170

saw me as some weak ass nigga who she could walk all over, but at this point, I wasn't concerned about that. I needed to help her get to safety so she could go on with her life and I could go on with mine.

I checked my gas level. "Listen, I'll take you to your sister tonight. I don't feel comfortable with y'all staying at my house."

Jazzmyne reeled as if I had slapped her. "We can't stay at your house?"

I scrunched my face up. "No! Have you forgotten our history?"

"I understand that, but..."

"No, you really don't seem to understand at all. In what world would you think it was okay to just stay at my house like nothing happened?"

Jazzmyne calmed. "Look, I don't want to fight with you, but I also don't want to show up at my sister's house looking like this." She gestured toward her ripped shirt and bloodstained jeans. "Can I at least change at your house before we drive out there?"

Jazzmyne's sister lived two hours away in a neighboring state.

I calculated in my mind. Did I really wanna have her in my apartment? The obvious answer was no, but at the same time, I could understand her desire to want to change clothes.

"Shit," I swore under my breath, then headed to my apartment.

We pulled up and I almost forgot Tremaine and Los were following. I was glad they came, because they could keep watch outside while I ensured Jazzmyne didn't try anything funny at my place.

Not that I thought she would, but there was no way I could trust her after what she had done to me.

I briefly explained the situation to my boys and they agreed to stay outside and keep watch. Jazzmyne, Kanai, and I went inside.

Chapter 29: Kyanah

After I got off the phone with Kaliss, I grew restless. My mind was on Kendrix and how he turned me on with everything he had done for my birthday.

At first, I was just going to go to sleep, but lustfulness got the best of me and I found myself throwing on a nightie and stilettos underneath a black trench coat, then grabbing my keys to head to his place.

Hopefully he wasn't already sleeping. Once he took one look at me, he would know what time it was.

Pulling down his street, a nervous feeling swept through me. What if he rejected me? We had vowed to take it slow.

At the same time though, we had been together a couple months. Why not take it to the next level? Especially since it was my birthday.

When I arrived at his apartment, I saw his car parked outside, but it looked like someone was in the front passenger seat.

At first, I thought it might have been Tremaine or Los, but as I stepped out of my car to approach the vehicle, I saw it was a woman.

She stared at me like she was wondering what I was doing at Kendrix's apartment.

I froze, then looked from her to Kendrix's apartment. His front door was open. I wanted to go to his door but first I needed to know who this woman was.

"Hello," I said as I approached her, trying to think if I remembered her from somewhere. "Who are you?"

"Who am I?" Her head snapped back. "The better question is, who are you?"

I stared her down. "I'm Kendrix's girlfriend."

She leveled me with a glare. "Well, that's funny, because I'm Kendrix's girlfriend."

"Excuse me?"

At that moment, Kendrix walked outside with a little boy who was wearing one of his shirts. The boy looked at me in fear and Kendrix's eyes widened with surprise. "Kyanah?"

The woman in the car cocked her head to the side. "Is this why you didn't want to let us in your house, Kendrix? You got some bird coming to see you?"

"Bird?" I repeated, stepping toward the car, and Kendrix rushed between us.

This felt like deja vu. My mind began swimming and I stepped back, my limbs suddenly shaky.

Kendrix addressed the woman. "Look I don't know what the fuck you got going on, Jazzmyne, but Kyanah is my woman."

"She's your woman, huh?" Jazzmyne said with attitude. "If you and her are so close, why did you come rushing over to get me?"

Kendrix fell silent, and I stared between him and the woman, who I just learned was Jazzmyne. Judging from the presence of the little boy, her and Kanai were just inside Kendrix's apartment.

"I need to leave," I said, stumbling backward, then turning to go to my car.

"Baby, wait!" Kendrix said, but his words fell on deaf ears.

Chapter 30: Kendrix

Kyanah peeled off before I could tell her what was going on. My heart sank as her car disappeared. I turned to Jazzmyne.

"What the hell did you just do?"

"What do you mean, what did I do? Was she the reason you didn't want us in your apartment?" Jazzmyne was demanding answers like she was my woman instead of Kyanah.

"Look Jazzmyne, I don't know what caused you to think that you have any level of control or say-so in my life but let me set you straight: all I'm doing is bringing you to the bus station. We'll just have to trust that you'll get to your sister safely."

Jazzmyne's jaw dropped. "What? You're not driving us out there?"

Her incredulous stare was blowing me. Who the hell did this woman think she was? She was delusional for thinking I was still going to drive her two hours away after the stunt she just pulled with Kyanah.

"I was going to bring you there, but that was before you tried to fuck up my relationship with my girl. Matter of fact, fuck that, I'm about to call you an Uber."

"Kendrix, we don't have any money for a bus ticket!" Her eyes welled with tears.

I stared at her for a second, this night growing worse the more time I spent in Jazzmyne's presence. So not only was she trying to stay at my house, she also had no money for her escape? I opened my mouth to ask what happened to her job, but that was none of my business. I needed to get rid of her before anything worse happened.

I looked at Kanai in the back seat. He was the innocent one in all this. I sighed. "Jazzmyne, I'm going to bring you to the bus station and pay for two one-way tickets for you and Kanai to get to your sister. Once I do that, I don't ever want to hear from you again. Don't call me or text me. I'm blocking you."

"Kendrix..."

"That's the best I can do."

She didn't respond, so I climbed in my driver's seat, wanting nothing more than to go to see Kyanah and explain what really happened.

But if Kanai was in danger, I couldn't let nothing happen to him.

We drove in silence to the bus station, where I paid for their bus tickets, and, against my better judgment, I gave Jazzmyne a couple hundred dollars for the road.

"Don't go back to that nigga, Jazzmyne, and please don't ever call me again," I warned.

She nodded and swiped a tear from her cheek, looking at me like she just lost the love of her life. Her delusion was starting to bother me, but I kept a tough exterior. I didn't know what she thought she was trying to pull with Kyanah, but now I had to go fix that mess.

First, I had to say goodbye to Kanai though.

I knelt to his level, much like I had the first time I saw him. "Hey little man," I said.

He was still staring at me blankly and it pained my heart.

"You're gonna be okay, you hear me?" I said.

Kanai was staring blankly at first, but then he focused on me and nodded.

That felt like a breakthrough.

Relief filled my veins. "You be good with your mother and auntie, stay in school, and get good grades, okay?"

Kanai nodded and a tear slipped down his cheek. I wished I could take him with me, but Jazzmyne's brother in law was a good dude. I trusted he would take care of the little man while Jazzmyne got on her feet.

"I'll see you around, okay?" I said, not wanting to say goodbye.

"Bye Kendrix," his little voice cracked, and I almost lost it.

I nodded and walked away from them, refusing to look back and become overrun by emotion.

Chapter 31: Kyanah

I barely made it to my apartment before I broke down in tears.

There I was sitting against my living room wall in a nightie and stilettos, looking dumb as hell, bawling my eyes out.

How could Kendrix do that to me?

When he told me the story of what happened between him and Jazzmyne, I thought that was a bonding moment for us. I thought I had met a man who could fully understand my pain, because he went through the same thing I did. And now he had played me just like Terrance.

After all the happiness of my birthday, now I was left with pain.

This seemed to be my lot in life.

Now that the same thing had happened to me twice, I was done with relationships altogether. They just weren't for me.

Inching to my feet, I was about to take off my silly ass outfit when my doorbell buzzed. Who the hell was buzzing me at this hour? It better not be Kendrix.

I stalked over, ready to give him a piece of my mind. "Hello?" I said after pressing the Talk button.

"Baby..." His voice strained through the intercom. "Can you please buzz me in?"

I buzzed without answering, then waited with my arms crossed for him to get to my apartment.

As soon as he got to the door, I wrenched it open and slapped him across the face.

"What the hell was that for?" he said, grabbing his jaw.

"That's for being a fucking liar and a cheater! I thought you were different, Kendrix."

He tried to step toward me but I backed away. "Say whatever you have to say so you can get the hell out of my apartment."

Kendrix stared at me.

"Kyanah..." He sighed.

"I'm waiting." I was tapping my foot against the floor, my body was so full of tension.

"Please just hear me out."

"I said I was listening."

He stared at me. "Look, I don't know what Jazzmyne said to you before me and Kanai walked out of my apartment, but whatever it was, she lied. After I got home and took my shower, Jazzmyne called my phone nine times out of the blue. At first, I wasn't going to answer, but then she texted me saying that her and Kanai were in danger."

As he spoke, he held out his phone for me to see. He showed me his call log, then the text message Jazzmyne had sent. I noted the fact that the thread was empty besides that message.

"Let me see your phone," I said, and grabbed it from him and went to his deleted folder. Although Kendrix and I hadn't officially said we were boyfriend and girlfriend, I considered us a couple and from the way he acted, he felt the same. He didn't protest or try to take his phone back. I scanned the screen. There were no threads between him and Jazzmyne there. Next, I scrolled his call log and saw no other calls besides tonight.

Lastly, I went to his social media and saw that she wasn't even his friend. I clicked her profile anyway to see if they exchanged any messages and there weren't any. I blocked her on social media, then from his phone as well before handing it back to him.

Then I urged him to continue the story. "Okay, so she called you and then what?"

He launched into it, highlighting how she kept begging to stay at his house but he didn't want her to, then she begged to go to his house to change. From the sounds of it, if he was telling the truth, Jazzmyne was trying to wrench her way back into his life. When he told the part about Tremaine and Los following him, I cut in.

"Tremaine and Los weren't at your apartment when I got there." I stared at him like I caught him in a lie.

Kendrix didn't flinch. "They left right before you arrived, I swear. I would never cheat on you, Kyanah. Please believe me."

Deep down in my heart, I believed him, but I needed more. "Are Tremaine and Los home now?"

He nodded like he wasn't following. "They should be, why?"

"Give me your phone. I'll be right back."

He scrunched his face. "Why do you want my phone?"

"Because I don't want you calling or texting them telling them to corroborate your story." I held my hand out for the phone.

Kendrix looked at me like he had been stung. "You have that low trust in me that you have to verify with my boys?"

"This is for my peace of mind, Kendrix. You know what the fuck I've been through."

He stared at me.

Then I started to feel like I was overstepping my bounds. We had been seeing each other for months, but we hadn't made it official. Maybe I was the only one who saw us as boyfriend and girlfriend, despite how he always acted.

I was about to open my mouth to say never mind, when Kendrix's expression softened.

He handed me the phone. "Knock yourself out. I'll be on the couch."

I wasn't sure if I should proceed. "No, never mind," I said, and handed it back toward him but he didn't take it.

"Do what you gotta do, Kyanah. I understand how you feel. I want this thing between me and you to work. If you need to go talk to Tremaine and Los to verify, go do that. I don't have shit to hide."

His tone was biting like he was upset again, but at the same time, it seemed like he really wanted me to go.

So I did.

I exited my apartment and strode to the elevator like I was on a mission. It wasn't until I got to Tremaine and Los' apartment that I realized I was still wearing my trench coat with barely anything else underneath.

Tremaine opened the door when I knocked. "Kyanah? What are you doing here?" He asked, a confused expression on his face.

I didn't answer his question. Instead, I asked one of my own. "Were you just with Kendrix?"

His eyes narrowed. "Yeah, why? Did something happen?"

I stared at him. "Did you see his ex, Jazzmyne?"

Tremaine didn't flinch. "Yeah, her man beat her ass so she called Kendrix to come get her. He called me and Los in case they were on some funny shit. But from what I understand he was taking her to her sister's house."

Up to that point in the story, I wasn't entirely sure why I came to Tremaine's door with this drama, but what he had just told me gave me the confirmation I needed to hear. If Tremaine was still under the impression that Kendrix was on the way to Jazzmyne's sister's house, that meant they hadn't spoken since the incident between me, him, and Jazzmyne.

Now I could rest.

"Thank you," I said.

"Is everything okay?" Los called out from the couch, where he was laying down.

Tremaine looked concerned too, and now I felt like a fool for interrogating them.

"Yes, everything's good. Kendrix is actually downstairs in my apartment. He's fine."

"Okay..." Tremaine still looked confused.

"Thank you. I'll see you guys later," I said, then exited their apartment.

As I walked down the hall toward the elevator, one of the phones buzzed in my trench coat pocket. I took it out when I got on the elevator. It was Kendrix's phone.

Tremaine had texted him. *Yo, what's up with Kyanah? Are you and her good? She just came to our apartment asking what happened.*

Re-entering my apartment, I approached Kendrix, who was sitting on my couch in the dark with his arms crossed.

"Find what you were looking for?" he asked with a stony expression.

I handed him his phone. "I had to be sure, Kendrix."

"Sure of what? Have I ever given you a reason to doubt me?"

"No, you haven't, but you know what I've been through. Plus, you just urged me to go. If you didn't want me to, why did you tell me to go up there?"

"The fact that you took me up on it shows that you don't trust me."

"Like I said before, it's not that I don't trust you, Kendrix, it's..."

"What is it then?" He turned in his seat, facing me squarely. "How else would you explain it other than a lack of trust."

I didn't want to argue with him now that I knew the truth, but we needed to have this conversation. "I didn't want to be hurt again."

He stood. "And when have I ever shown you that I would be the nigga to hurt you?"

"You haven't, but things could easily change."

"So you don't believe I'm serious about you."

"Terrance acted serious too, and look where that got me."

"I ain't Terrance."

As soon as he said those words, they broke something within me. The final doubt that I had been holding onto about whether Kendrix was really for me or whether he would end up hurting me all over again.

"I'm sorry."

He stared at me, his expression still etched in stone.

I persisted. "Seriously, Kendrix. I mean it. I know I just made you feel like I don't trust you, but I wasn't being fair to you. You haven't been anything but solid since we met."

His expression softened. "You're good. I understand how you might have jumped to conclusions in the heat of the moment."

I nodded and held his gaze, hoping that this wouldn't drive a wedge between us.

He fell silent as if contemplating my words, then he relaxed his arms, looking up at me, then down my body.

"Why did you come to my apartment tonight anyway?"

I didn't want to tell him because now I felt like an idiot, but I felt like I at least owed him an explanation.

"I came to surprise you."

"With what?" he joked, seeming like he was putting two and two together. "You hiding a gun underneath that trench coat?"

I undid the belt part, then the buttons, letting it hit the floor. "No, I was hiding this." Now that I was standing before him, showing my intentions for how I originally wanted my night to end, I was once again in a vulnerable position. He could turn me down like last time, and if he did, I couldn't even blame him after the mini-argument we just had.

Kendrix's eyes widened at the sight of my nightie, then he stepped forward to approach me. "Well damn, I'm surprised."

I let out a rough chuckle. "Now it's ruined though."

He pulled me into his arms. "The night ain't over. Before all this went down, I was about to be on my way to you."

"Really?"

He nodded. "I been fiending for a minute to finish what we started."

There was no need for further explanation because I knew exactly what he was talking about.

We stared into each other's eyes, then Kendrix leaned down to kiss me. Despite my six-inch stilettos, he was still taller than me.

Soon, our slow, soulful kiss became filled with passion. I wanted to jump his bones and take my time, at the same time.

I was running my hands up and down his back and he was gripping my thighs. He lifted me off my feet and carried me to my bedroom, my heels falling off along the way. It felt like déjà vu, but I hoped it would have the opposite ending from last time we got this close.

When he laid me down and I felt his weight on top of me, my mind immediately went back to that night again. We weren't ready then, but tonight, hopefully, nothing was stopping us.

Kendrix began kissing my neck, licking and sucking like he had done before. I moaned his name, begging for more as my body heated with anticipation.

He lifted my nightie, and I wasn't wearing a bra or panties underneath.

"Damn," he murmured, when I was completely naked before him. Then his kisses trailed to my nipples, ensuring that each was given ample attention. He drove me crazy, flickering his tongue back and forth in a rapid fashion.

"Kendrix, oh my…"

I willed him to go lower, and as if he heard my thoughts, he did.

Kendrix's kisses trailed down my belly, then he swirled his tongue around my belly button, causing my excitement to build even stronger. I spread my legs wide and he parted my lips with his fingers before sliding his tongue up and down my clit.

Within seconds, my legs were trembling because it had been so long since anyone had been down there and Kendrix was an expert compared to Terrance. He was doing shit with his tongue that should have been illegal, the way it drove me crazy.

He was licking my pussy like his life depended on it, then when my body shuddered with the impending explosion, he didn't let up until he had licked every drop of my juices.

I had never cum like that before in my life.

I lay there, breathless and speechless, as Kendrix made his way back up my body. "How was that?" he asked with a smirk, and I couldn't even answer.

He allowed me to cool down before he began licking and sucking on my neck again, then playing with my kitty. Pretty soon, I was hot and ready all over again.

I felt his size up against me and I was almost afraid to do more, but at the same time, this was the moment I had been waiting for.

Kendrix gently eased his way in, allowing me to adjust to his size and girth. Then he stared into my eyes as he slow-stroked me to oblivion.

Chapter 32: Kendrix

Me, Kyanah, Tremaine, Kaliss, Tracey, and Los embarked on a cruise to Cuba. Kyanah and her sister were originally supposed to go alone, but when Kaliss announced that she and Tremaine had made their relationship official, Kyanah immediately updated the plans.

That sneaky nigga. Tremaine had kept silent about his and Kaliss' relationship, never saying shit to me or Los about it, though we both knew they were seeing each other.

"You better treat her right too," I warned, the night Tremaine finally came out and said she was his girl. Tremaine was known to fuck em and duck em. I didn't doubt his intentions toward Kyanah's sister, but I had to be sure.

"Chill bro, it's not even like that," he said, and I could tell by the way he was cheesing he was serious about Kaliss.

I was glad to see that.

I never thought I would sue the day when Tremaine would settle down, but it seemed like he was moving in that direction.

Los and Tracey had been going strong for a minute too, though Los hadn't mentioned wanting to take things to the next level of getting engaged.

As for me, on the other hand...

I had met the love of my life. With Jazzmyne, I thought I had something special, but when I met Kyanah, everything fell into place.

Despite the ups and downs we went through when getting to know each other, there was something about her that I couldn't shake.

From the way things had been progressing between us, she felt the same.

We had only been together nine months, but I figured, why wait? It wasn't going to take me ten years to know if I had the right woman when she was standing right in front of me staring in my face.

Kyanah had no clue, but I was hopefully about to make her three carats richer. I hoped she said yes.

We partied on the cruise like there was no tomorrow, visiting all the tourist spots and eating all the good food. The women forced us into countless selfies and group photos every step of the way, and we pretended not to enjoy it while secretly counting our blessings.

But on the final night, it was my time to shine.

We were sitting at a candlelit table distanced from all the others. It was a couple's cruise, so each couple had their own table, but I had the most beautiful woman on the ship sitting right across from me.

"This night couldn't be more perfect," Kyanah breathed, then stared up at the starry sky. It reminded me of other nights we would spend together, staring up at the sky and talking about life at the end of a romantic date.

"You sure about that?" I asked, and she turned back to face me with a question in her eyes, but I rose from my seat, slowly making my way toward her and pulling the ring box from my pocket.

"Kendrix, what are you doing?" Kyanah asked, her eyes widening and face flushing with nervousness.

"What you think?" I said with a cocky grin. "I'm snatching you off the market."

I knelt before her and opened the ring box as her eyes filled with tears.

"Kendrix, it's beautiful."

I stared up into her eyes. "Kyanah, you are the most beautiful woman I have ever encountered. I know we haven't been together that long, but since the moment I met you, you have deeply impacted my life. We started off on bad footing, but there was always something about you that drew me in. We've both been through some situations that caused us heartache and pain, but I want to spend the rest of my days turning your frown upside down. When I look at you, I see my future. I wanna be the reason you smile. Will you marry me?"

Kyanah became overcome with emotion and covered her lips with a trembling hand, blinking back happy tears.

She nodded, fanning her face, and my heart swelled with joy.

Though I loved her and I knew she loved me, we had only been together nine months. Many would say that that was too soon to know you had the one, especially considering our pasts. But I knew what I felt when I thought of Kyanah, and it filled my heart with excitement to know that she felt the same. I slid the ring on her finger and helped her to her feet for a hug and kiss.

Light applause broke out around us, but my mind wasn't on them. It was as if the boat, the staff, and the other patrons had disappeared. Kyanah was the only thing that mattered.

Epilogue: Kendrix

One year later...

The night Kyanah said yes was the happiest night of my life.

We had only been married six months but I already knew we were counting down to forever. After our wedding night, Kyanah wanted to move in with me, but I didn't feel like an apartment would suit her. I wanted the first place we lived in together to be a house.

So she planned the wedding while I continued saving and busting my ass to close on a three bedroom home before our wedding date.

We barely saw each other during the process, but it was worth it. I held her down and she held me down too, like it was supposed to be.

After our honeymoon to Tahiti, we moved into our home. Kyanah and I wanted three bedrooms to accommodate our two children we hoped to have.

Ironically, the night we got engaged, Los planned to propose to Tracey too. As much as he complained about her cooking, he could never get enough of that girl. Thankfully, she said yes to him too, so we had two weddings to look forward to.

Los and Tracey got married a week before us and waited to go on their honeymoon until after our wedding.

Tremaine and Kaliss were still taking things slow, as me and Kyanah had planned to do with our relationship before we realized we had something real, but I personally believed Tremaine was head over heels despite being terrified of marriage.

Sooner or later, my boy would come around.

"Babe!" Kyanah called out as the front door slammed and she entered the house from work. I exited our bedroom and went to the top of the stairs to approach her.

She beamed up at me from where she stood.

"Guess what?"

My heart thumped in my chest. Something told me this was the news we had been waiting on. Others had told us to wait, but Kyanah and I didn't see the point in waiting when we both knew what we wanted.

"What is it?" I asked, fighting back a smile.

She tapped her purse and gestured for me to come downstairs. "Come and see."

I descended the circular staircase and met my wife at the bottom. I had a feeling what it was, but I wanted to see it for myself.

Opening her purse, Kyanah pulled out something thin and tubular that was wrapped in tissue paper.

I unwrapped it to find a pregnancy test.

Two lines.

"We're pregnant!" she blurted, smiling from ear to ear, then she flung her arms around me while I stood in stunned silence.

I had already known what was going to happen, but now that I saw it, I couldn't believe my eyes. Kanai had been wrenched from my life from circumstances out of my control. Losing him had hurt me in ways I couldn't describe. But now, the pain I felt from the abrupt ending of me and Kanai's relationship was alleviated. I was going to have a son or daughter of my own.

Epilogue: Kyanah

Another three years...

It turned out that Kendrix and I didn't have to wait to have our two children. They both came at once.

We named our son Kendrix Jr. and our daughter was named after Kaliss.

"Damn, y'all couldn't call her Tremaine'a?" Tremaine said when we shared the news, and he looked dead serious too.

We all burst out laughing, but he held his stance.

"I'm being for real! The boy, I could see him being a junior, but I'm the one who hooked y'all up. Babe, see how they played me?" He looked at Kaliss, who cocked her head.

"Boy, how did they play you when they named my niece after me?"

Tremaine stared at her for a moment before he broke character and started laughing too.

I was happy how my life was turning out.

Kendrix and I were going strong, and so were Los and Tracey and Tremaine and Kaliss. My sister had held out hope for relationships while I had almost given up, but now we both had good men in our lives.

Life was sweet.

We all gathered around for a Thanksgiving feast, which was hosted at our house this year. Beverly attended, and she, Kaliss and I did the cooking while Tracey made the sweets. Los, Tremaine, and Kendrix did nothing but watch football in the living room and complain about the food taking too long.

When we finished cooking, we sat around the table with the kids at their kiddie table off to the side of the kitchen. Our son and daughter were sitting with Los and Tracey's daughter, Lourdes.

Kendrix said grace and we all dug in.

Halfway through the meal, Tremaine shot out of his seat.

His movement was so fast, it startled everyone, and Los started choking on his food. "What the hell is wrong with you, man?" Los said, and Tremaine looked solemn for a second before he cracked a smile.

"Nothing." His grin widened, then he pretended like he was about to sit back down but swerved in Kaliss' direction instead. She was sitting next to him.

"Tremaine, stop playing," she said, irritated at his antics at first, until he got down on bended knee and pulled out the ring box.

Her eyes widened and her head whipped toward me, but I was already recording the moment on my phone.

"Awww!" everyone said as my sister burst into tears and accepted her ring.

I wiped tears from my eyes too after the moment was over.

Now our circle was complete.

The End

Dear Reader,

I hope you enjoyed my debut! Kendrix and Kyanah went through a lot in their past relationships, but I was glad to see them find love together in the end. How about you? Did you enjoy reading about this couple?

If so, I would love to hear your thoughts in a rating or review. Reviews give books exposure so Kendrix and Kyanah's story can get into more readers' hands.

Don't be shy – I wanna hear from you!

To connect with me in other ways, check out my newsletter and socials:

Newsletter: https://author-nisha.ck.page/authornisha
Tiktok: @author.nisha
Instagram: @authornisha_blklove

Facebook: Author NISHA
Gmail: nishatheauthor@gmail.com
Amazon: NISHA

I would love to hear from you. Thank you for reading :)

Made in United States
Troutdale, OR
08/24/2024